The Rabbit Saga Collection

Darcy Vandiver
Vampire Sexpert

a memoir

emil jersey

The Rabbit Saga Collection

Darcy Vandiver Vampire Sexpert, A Memoir
By Emil Jersey
First Edition, ©2020 Emil Jersey

FIRST EDITION V.04242021
Also available in Kindle eBook
ISBN 978-1-7340474-5-5

Run Rabbit Books
A Division of Little Roni Publishers, LLC
www.littleronipublishers.com/run-rabbit-books.php

Licensed Cover Image © Innervision/DepositPhotos.com
Cover Design: Elizabeth E. Little, Hyliian Graphics
Photo of Jersey (Licensed) www.depositphotos.com /Rdrgraphe

"Emil Jersey" is a collaborative effort nom de plume consisting of Emil Stern, DH Lee, and EC Maze. Emil Stern writes under many pen names with thousands of fan-fiction followers. His first original novel is from Run Rabbit Books, "Blood, Sex & Violence, A Vampire's Rebuttal," which chronicles choice characters from the Rabbit Saga Collection. Follow Emil Jersey at www.emiljersey.com

PUBLISHED IN THE UNITED STATES OF AMERICA

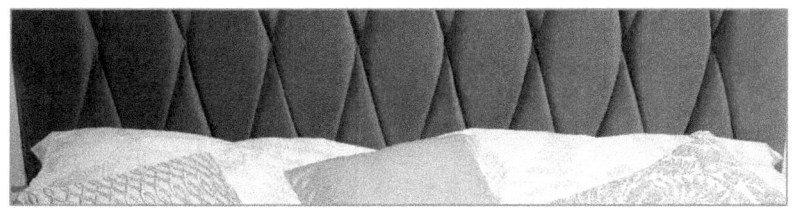

This Series Includes the Following:

The Rabbit Saga, Books 1-5, by Ellen C. Maze

RABBIT: CHASING BETH RIDER (1)
RABBIT LEGACY (2)
RABBIT REDEMPTION (3)
ANOMALY: BEYOND THE RABBIT (4)
CONUNDRUM: THE LOST RABBIT (5)
VESTIGE: FATHERS & DAUGHTERS (6)

The Rabbit Saga Collection by Emil Jersey
(May be read in any order)

BLOOD, SEX & VIOLENCE by Emil Jersey
MALCONTENT by Emil Jersey
DARCY VANDIVER, VAMPIRE SEXPERT, A
MEMOIR by Emil Jersey

Publisher's note: More to be added, visit the author's website to sign up for alerts, or follow the author on Amazon for email alerts of new releases.

Rabbit Saga   ellencmaze.com
Rabbit Saga Collection   emiljersey.com

From the Author
About Brother Darcy, Sexy Af
Jersey

MY NAME IS JERSEY AND I WAS BORN IN 1699.
Run Rabbit Books published my bestselling memoir last year under the title, "Blood, Sex & Violence, a Vampire's Rebuttal." It is now time to tell you about my very favorite and most compatible Rakum brother, Darcy Vandiver. As you'll soon read, our specialty is **sexually servicing our Elders** (and we fix anyone else we choose for our own kicks).

IN 2018, OUR WORLD WENT TO SHIT.
We are *Rakum*, a legitimate race of supernatural demigods that live, play, and feed, under the radar of humankind. There used to be 100,000 brethren across the globe, where now, we have less than ten thousand. Eight years ago, because of events chronicled in this series (The Rabbit Saga), every single Rakum brother turned human outside of our control. We hate it, but you know the saying: **assimilate or murder everyone around you.**

In the very back of this book, I included a truncated version of this chapter from my book—the night Jersey went human. Oh, it was awful, and the timing could not have been worse—Avi was just about to rock my world. *Shit!* Anyway, proceed to Darcy's book if you prefer. Either way, you will love it all.

And at any rate, I may be mortal, but Rakum are still superior.
And sexy.
And fun.

SO… LET'S GET STARTED.

Darcy Vandiver, like me, is ish-mikhan from birth, and he's the only Rakum I would consider my equal. He's sexy AF and when he submitted these chapters, I must have read them a dozen times. They are as delicious as he is. Read on and enjoy.

PS: The tales of our people are told in various volumes under The Rabbit Saga and The Rabbit Saga Collection.

~ Jersey

"Take it away, polsc'v'."~ Jersey

"Kazak, Jerz. This will be fun…"   ~ Darcy

(©Licensed Author Photos, *polsc'v'*, Rakum Hungarian, means "favored one". *Kazak* is the Rakum greeting, means, "Be Strong.")

Your Delicious Chapters

1

I Gave Him My Heart

THESE FACTS I HOLD AS TRUTH: A VAMPIRE memoir should start with the drinking of blood. How then, shall a vampire "sexpert's" tale begin? Sex? I shall give you both. Also, when I had completed my chapters, I decided to pull out my favorite for the start of the book. I'm confident you will enjoy it as much as I enjoyed living it (the balance of the telling will occur more or less chronologically).

I came into the world in 1710, born a Rakum (you would call us "vampires"), and at age nine, my masters discovered I was born "ish-mikhan," a Rakum word for "fix-it man." This meant I possessed innate skill in the ways of sexually pleasing my Elders. But more on that in subsequent chapters.

1

I was favored and spoiled in every assignment but allow me to share on my favorite topic: Elder Canaan. This event occurred in 1932, when I met the master I would hold in my heart for the rest of my days. Jersey wrote about it from Canaan's perspective in his memoir, *Blood, Sex & Violence, A Vampire's Rebuttal* and now you shall see what I was thinking when this amazing man entered my timeline.[1] Please, allow me to tell you how it really went.

Ken and Yan had been assigned to the Elder as soldiers, and although I was a captain by then and outranked them, Elder Bel, my master, assured me my role was to be strictly sexual. He held an affinity for Elder Canaan and enjoyed his company when we gathered. One thing he shared was that Canaan had little interest in fucking, no matter who offered; he had reached an age where he'd rather fight than anything else. Bel told me, "He had a valet before he graduated to Elder and you remind me of him. Not in looks—Judas Priest, no one looks like Darcy Vandiver—but in personality, joviality, likable nature. If Canaan sees you and doesn't instantly bend you over, he'll do it shortly after. He will not be able to resist you. And Darcy, listen. I want you to lay it on heavy. This Elder needs to breathe

---

[1] Here is a secret link for my readers who might like to read that chapter for free online. https://www.emiljersey.com/Canaan-meets-Darcy-from-BSV.php

this aura you exude. Do you understand?"

I assured Master Bel that I would do as he instructed and me and my two escorts headed away. The trip was long and when we reached the city, we ducked into a Rakum waystation to freshen up. Ken and Yan spent most of the journey pretending I wasn't there, which was fine with me. They hadn't been instructed to stay off the ish-mikhan; it was their choice. Because of their indifference, by the time we reached the safehouse, I'd gone seventy-two hours without sex. This was on my mind as Ken walked ahead of me through the double doors of the building.

"There's a brother here named Geoffrey. He'll fuck you," Yan said as he passed my position and disappeared with Ken into the hall and out of sight. I stood in the center of the main room, sniffing out the shower since those two assholes didn't bother to help me find it.

Geoffrey…

I hadn't heard of him. I inhaled again, sorting the aromas, my own being the most offensive. I needed to wash and fast. Elder Canaan expected us soon and an ish-mikhan should never be late. I chose a hallway that smelled most of bleach and headed down. A shower started up and I realized I had chosen well. I reached a closed door and pushed it open.

"Kazak,"[2] the brother in the shower called without knowing who had entered. The steam prevented me from seeing his face and I called a greeting as I peeled off my shirt. There was one shower head, so the guy would need to get out or share. Before you ponder too long, Rakum are raised communally; we ate, slept, and bathed together since we were weaned. For this reason, the brother in the shower did not turn as he heard me clomp off my shoes and slide open the glass door to join him in the tight space. There was enough room for two, but not three.

"I'm done, just had to rinse off," the guy said and moved aside for me to take the lead.

Because of my nature, I looked upon him as I scooched around. He wasn't quite six feet, with bronzed skin, black hair and a razor-thin mustache. He raised his eyes to mine—deep brown, almost black, in a handsome, chiseled face. I felt my grin tuck into my cheek and he reflected the move.

"A fix-it man," he said as a statement and stopped the effort of leaving the stall. He squared up and took his time considering me from chin to toes. "Can you read grunts or just Elders?"

My smile widened because what I read was extremely interesting. Not only had Geoffrey been with ish-mikhan, he'd been with Jersey. And *a lot*. If you

---

[2] Rakum greeting, means literally, "be strong."

haven't read Jersey's memoir, I'll clue you in—Jersey mentored me. My first Elder held me close until I was seventy and then he sent me off to Elder Emil. The way the world works, on the way to Emil, my trip was hijacked by another Elder—Master Kilmeade—who we all considered the greatest of all Elders. He took me to his estate where he put me with his ish-mikhan, Jersey. He wanted to see if we would be compatible. Judas Priest, were we compatible! *Fuck!* (I promise; you'll hear more on this later in the book)

When I looked into Geoffrey's mind and saw Jersey, I went on full-staff. He noticed and grinned. With nonchalance, his right hand took hold of my erection. In the first two seconds, I recognized the move he applied. Without going into too much detail, suffice it to say there are ways to move one's fingers on a circumcised man, and Geoffrey had been instructed well. Rakum grunts retain their foreskin (only the Fathers, Elders and ish-mikhan are circumcised) so his amazing skill meant Jersey spent a good amount of time explaining how to please.

"You like that," Geoffrey said and stepped closer as if to ask for a kiss.

I allowed him to get right under my nose, the hot water jets slamming my back and then I shook my head. "I'm on a mission, brother," I told him in my sexiest voice. "But you can wash me. I'd like that."

I wasn't asking. It's complicated to mortals, but several things were going on at the same time. I'll break it down for you because I want to, and this is my book. Geoffrey had been spoiled by Jersey, and his technique, no matter how flawless, could not make up for his arrogance. Add to that, I outranked him. Geoffrey wasn't a soldier, and I was, so I was his master. *Also,* I was a century older, which also made me his master. On top of all that, I hadn't been instructed to pleasure the guy. I considered all this as he pondered his next move. I knew what I wanted. My muse, the ish-mikhan spirit inside, wanted this condescending ass-wipe to bathe me. He was going to *please me.* I waited, another moment passed, and he finally slow-blinked.

"Your will is my will," Geoffrey said holding my eye, his delightful massage leaving my member to reach for the soap. For the next eleven minutes, Geoffrey of the South Street Waystation washed the fix-it man, and since I was being prepared to visit an Elder, he took extra care with every element of his duty. When I was as clean as a man can be, he shut off the water and stood facing me, both of us dripping and I expected him to commence the toweling off. Instead, he asked, "Will you be sleeping here when you finish with the Elder? I'll watch for you."

"This is outside of my control, but feel free to wait,"

I said. I needed to turn the blade. I mean, he'd been such a cocky prick—grunts are supposed to *venerate* me, not work an angle to get me to bed. I brought my hands up to frame his face, and this is the first time I'd touched him. His eyes grew soft and he parted his lips.

"Yes?" he whispered.

"If I come back here, I'll sleep in your quarters and show you everything Jersey held back. How does that sound?" I dug around in his gaze until we locked eyes hard and he could not look away. He also couldn't speak, his body online in a heartbeat. I waited another long second and kissed his forehead before leaving the stall. I did not allow him to towel me and I left the room, naked and dripping water. Was it showy? Yes. Was it cruel? I'd say so. I walked to the main room and called for my escorts to bring a towel along with my clothes. They did so after a minute and down the hallway, Geoffrey worked out his love pain all by himself.

"Darcy, you're such a shit," Yan said as I dried off and then reached for the dress slacks he held out. The three of us would present ourselves to the unfamiliar Elder in our best suits and my two escorts were clean, dressed, and had fed on some Cow[3] I never saw, distracted as I had been with Geoff.

---

[3] "Cow," a mortal viscerally drawn to give over his or her blood and body to my people.

"I am what I am," I whispered with a sideways smile. Yan had never met Elder Kilmeade, but this was his signature phrase and those of us who knew him loved to repeat it. I slipped on the Egyptian cotton shirt, and once buttoned, I flipped the tailored coat over one arm. "I'm ready."

"About damn time," Ken complained from the door. He clicked his tongue and we followed him out.

I took my place in the backseat, enjoying the sensation of being chauffeured. The two soldiers didn't mind; they enjoyed their job and they enjoyed each other. This is why they found it so easy to resist their beautiful companion. I watched them send each other laughing glances and secret nods like shit-eating mortals. Their behavior would have an Elder in fits of rage, but I wouldn't tell. I rarely saw such affection between brothers and I let them have it, my mind on Elder Canaan.

I had asked around once I knew we were headed to his abode. His reputation was one of bullish, cantankerous provocation. This didn't faze me—how many Elders were gentle kittens? *Zero.* Every grunt I questioned said Canaan smashed them, and not only that, but once smashed, he ground them into the dirt with his heel. I also loved violence—especially before sex. This caused me to smile, and Ken, who piloted us through the dark streets, caught my movement in the rearview mirror.

"Check his lap. Shit, he's jumping out of his skin."

"Leave him alone—they love Elders," Yan said with a tiny glance my way. "Fucking fix-it men. I don't get it. The Elders? Shit."

I smiled and looked out the car window. Our population regarded the One Hundred Elders to be a posse of gigantic assholes. But the ish-mikhan? These amazing leaders were my very *life*. They weren't like us, superior in every way, and only the Fathers and the ish-mikhan could see this. At any rate, Ken was right. I *was* counting the minutes.

Elder Canaan…

He was said to be big and muscled, but not enormous like Elder Bel. Also, he had been proselytized by Elder Jack Dawn, so I could expect him to be especially pugilistic. I huffed to myself in the dark interior; I had only asked about him to tickle my anticipation. When my eyes landed in his, my muse (the ish-mikhan spirit inside of me) would tell me what to do. It was 100% reliable.

We finally arrived and headed up, the Elder residing in a tri-level apartment building. Mortals thought the rooms were inhabited by their kind, but in truth, only Rakum lived there. We don't trust humans to know where we sleep, so the place was heavily barricaded during the day and all of my brethren slept below ground in a light-tight barricaded cellar.

This night, as we entered the ground floor front door, a brother met us and showed us to the receiving chamber. A door was yanked open to reveal a twelve-by-twelve foyer. Once Ken, Yan, and I entered, a soldier joined us from the inner rooms. He spoke to my escorts, but I don't know what he said. My mind had turned to Elder Canaan. I couldn't see him, and I didn't know his scent, but my muse had locked onto his thread causing my skin to twitch. My breath grew shallow and my pulse increased. The chatty-Cathy called Tork served as the Elder's top lieutenant and he soon stepped up to me, asking inane questions I ignored. He yammered on, teasing me, trying to draw my ire, and just before I squashed him for his impudence, he turned away, instructing us to wait to be called.

"The Fathers must think you're lonely..." That was Tork speaking to his master in the other room. I remained behind my escorts, but my muse sang louder in my ears.

"Send them in, idiot," the Elder replied, and Ken and Yan started forward.

My muse began stroking the master's psyche even before I met his eye, so when he saw me, we both felt as if we'd already met. How do I write how magnificent this man was to my eyes this night? I consider myself a decent wordsmith, but are there phrases in the English language to describe this moment? In Rakum Hungarian, I'd say, *l'plzc karn'v lolz,* a sentiment that means basically, *Darcy died and was brought back to life simply by connecting eyes with this master.*

Melodramatic, eh? As you'll learn, I'm a romantic. Jersey accused me of this more than once in his memoir. I accept it. And I accept that Elder Canaan had never had such a reaction to another person—human or Rakum. He held my gaze that first time only two seconds, but I read *volumes* in that moment. Canaan looked to my escorts and listened to them introduce me. I grinned when he fought the urge to look my way. He found me goddamn gorgeous and he sent Ken and Yan off with Tork before they made note of his erection.

"Step up, asshole," he commanded when we were alone.

I wasted no time but got right into his face. If he'd have allowed it, I would have yanked him close—rough and mean—and pressed my mouth to his hard enough to bruise his lips. He read my mind and chuckled, so fucking handsome, shaking his head, his blonde curls bouncing with the move.

"You're not all that, jerkoff." He put one hand to my neck. "Show me your last assignment."

11

He wanted to see me with my brethren, and I thought of Elder Bel—of course, of the two of us in bed. Canaan smirked and a miniscule eye meet occurred before he wiggled his hand.

"Show me the most recent Assembly."

I was with Elder Tomás at that time and he watched the Elder interact with me and shuffle off. Tomás did not screw ish-mikhan. *To each his own,* I thought, and Master Canaan chuckled anew.

"Boo-hoo," he said teasing and finally met my eye for longer than a moment. "Did it hurt your feelings, little brother, that Tomás would rather eat shit than spend one more second in your presence?"

Holy shit, this was it. The time had arrived for me to please my master and I felt it to my bones. I followed my muse and responded, "Yes, Master, I cry myself to sleep every sunrise."

Oh, the fire in his eyes! Shit! In a heartbeat, this amazing master drew back and brutally punched my middle as hard as he possibly could. My body flew backward with the force of it and in my torso, my organs suffered varying ruptures. I landed on the sofa, semi-longways, so as the Elder approached to resume the attack, I lifted my legs and tucked my arms up to prop my head. My internal injuries were healing and I hid my discomfort enough to say in a silky voice, "That was beautiful, Master. Please, let's do it again."

"Narcissistic asshole son of a bitch!" he barked, half-grinning and he zoomed into me, grabbing my shirt by both lapels. He jerked upward and the material frayed to nothing.

I wish you could have seen his face, holding my shirt in his hand and gazing upon my naked chest—he looked like a man drinking water in a desert. He took a deep breath and then another, his eyes scanning me slowly and with intent. He blinked once, twice, and that dashing smile hit his lips again.

"Say it," he commanded, laugh-talking.

"Master?" I asked, teasing, reclined, splayed, my mind open and so available for whatever my master wanted.

"Say it, motherfucker," he said this time in a whisper, his shoulders dropping the tiniest bit.

I needed to be careful now. I had reached the point where an ish-mikhan can err. Elder Canaan had opened himself up to abuse, to disrespect. He liked me—and this was dangerous for him. I would say the words and we'd go somewhere private. He didn't need to publicly reveal weakness of any sort—even the kind directly associated with his dick.

"Whatever I have is yours," I said low and he chuckled with relief, lowered his head, and pointed to the hallway.

With levity I rolled off the couch to land on my knees and slowly stand tall. With a flirtatious glance, I turned and left the room, his eyes on me as heavily as hands. I heard him say to Tork, *"Do not disturb."* Then I was in his bedroom. I crossed to turn and face the door, standing square, and Master Canaan walked in, slamming the door behind him.

"Darcy fucking Vandiver," he said and came toward me half the distance. "Bel favors you…"

I held his eye and stepped closer stopping five feet away. He dug around in my mind, his mental fingers jerking my thread like a mean kid pulling ponytails.

"Kilmeade favors you," he said, impressed more than before. "You are truly special."

He had said the last in a whisper and I stepped into him following my muse. The fighting was done. This Elder needed fixing and this time, I used my hands. I opened his shirt and it fell to the smooth floor and then his belt. Canaan stood quietly, his arms at his sides, watching me, half-smiling. The Elder closed his eyes to my massage and I gently pressed him to back the three strides to the bed. He allowed me to lead, respecting my vocation, and he sank onto the mattress with an exhale, as if the weight of the world had lifted from his shoulders.

Then I was lying beside him, telling him how beautiful, matchless, and perfect he was, all the while my hands, mouth, and tongue worshipped him as he deserved. Before long, he uttered a word I treasure to this day (and no one else has ever called me by this name).

"Vanny," he said, the word leaving his lungs more than simply passing his vocal chords. *"Vanny, don't ever stop."*

Shit, I love that memory.

Elder Canaan didn't send me home the next night. Elder Bel missed me and he sent for us, but Ken and Yan left without the ish-mikhan. Master Canaan held me twelve weeks and I lived more in that time than I had in the centuries before it. Also, as this chapter is called, I gave him my heart. I'm writing this memoir in 2021 and I don't sleep with my brothers these days. Yet I still think about Elder Canaan. I guess I always will.

Ahhh…

You have been primed. Let us dive now into my memoir.

Blood, sex and violence. With Rakum, you get all three. I invite you into my tale, my long life as courtesan to my Elders and lover to my chosen brethren. If you are unfamiliar with my people, you only need to absorb the following paragraphs. Then, I invite you to dive in with both feet.

The Rakum (RAH'-kum) are a powerful vampire race. We have 10 Fathers (all ancient) and 100 Elders who serve as our leaders on the ground. The rest of us are grunts, 100,000 in total. All Rakum are male and if we're smart, we can live thousands of years. We live among you, hidden except from a select few.

In 2018, our race was turned mortal outside of our control. This memoir is about our time BEFORE that shitty night.[1]

As I established, I am ish-mikhan (a fix-it man), an expert in pleasure. Each Rakum youth discovers his key strength usually by age eight. From there, it is up to the group lair proctors to develop and hone these natural propensities until age thirteen when he is assigned an Elder who initiates First Ritual (a delightfully violent toughening process lasting up to ten years).[4] In any generation, less than one in a thousand are discovered to be *ish-mikhan*, so we are coveted among our race.

Wait, sex at age nine? Most humans prickle at the thought of sexual activity among the young. Jersey wrote about me in his memoir[5] sharing how I was nine before

---

[4] "For example, my favorite is "the Ritual of the Broken Bones." You're young, maybe 8 or 9 at this point of the Ritual, and your Elder breaks a bone to watch it heal. Once it reforms, he will break it again. This process is repeated multiple times nightly over a period of weeks until your body learns to repair itself in moments." ~ Darcy

[5] *Blood, Sex & Violence, A Vampire's Rebuttal* by Emil Jersey, Run Rabbit Books, 2019.

my masters identified me as ish-mikhan. Why? I was physically larger than the other youths, so a lair proctor with no reason to look deeper would rightly assume I was to be a soldier. As it turned out, I grew into an *awesome* soldier, reaching the rank of lieutenant in my prime. But what the proctor missed was that the tallest, strongest, and most comely proselyte in their midst was filled with the spirit of the ish-mikhan, and oh, how they later wished they'd known.

Most humans wonder, *can a seven, eight, or nine-year-old Rakum youth* **want** *to perform sexual acts?* The answer (and the explanation) lies in the question.

Mortals wonder about these things because they aren't Rakum. To our kind, sexual stimulation is no more sacred than a handshake, we have no hang ups, no labels, and no moral dilemma. Plus, *a Rakum serves*—from birth to death, we understand that in general, each of us serves whoever is older. Secondly, the ish-mikhan spirit has one goal—to see an Elder *satisfied.* Because of this single-minded nature of Rakum and the spirit inside of me, I was only happy when I made my master happy.

As you read on, remember that we're not human and are opposite you in many ways. As I mentioned, blood, sex, and violence are the Rakum's top priorities, and the order of go varies. With all of this in mind, get ready for a delightful vampire memoir. We'll pick up

17

where Jersey's "Rebuttal memoir" left off: when Elder
Pebb kicked me from the nest…

2

Built Like an Elder

UNTIL I WAS THIRTEEN, MY ELDER DWARFED ME, hulking much taller when I had earned an embrace, engulfing me when time to perform my duties as ish-mikhan. At twelve, I had reached six feet and still looked up when he came close. When I reached 6'3", we stood nose-to-nose and that is when Master Pebb began moving me aside in his heart. I felt this with my every cell and read it in his countenance. Because ish-mikhan are given leniency (our emotional state is more human than that of our brethren) I was not chastised when my gloomy attitude grew evident.

More human…

In Rakum vernacular, each brother is born of a breeder, a woman the Fathers chose for this purpose. No Rakum ever meets this female, meaning, no Rakum has a "mother." I explained that so you might appreciate why, as you read, I will seem more "human" than my brethren. Across our race, only the ish-mikhan are permitted even the slightest appearance of "weakness," (i.e. mortalness), and for us, it isn't weakness because it is our *power* to manipulate and control our brothers with our sexual allure. Granted, all of us are appealing to humans, but the ish-mikhan's strength is in controlling our empathetic impulses, channeling this "humanness" for our own gratification and to please our Elders. You won't hold it against me if I appear to "care" or "love" some brethren over the others. Remember, this is about me satisfying my muse. I'm an extremely powerful motherfucker, and I kick ass when appropriate (I'm a goddamn Rakum lieutenant!). But I'm always ish-mikhan first.

Back to Master Pebb sending me away.

I had turned seventy, which means he held me closer much longer than anyone expected. The night I was to depart, I awoke depressed. Tarn and Gilmore, my bedmates, were even more distraught and would miss me terribly. Yes, in bed we performed flawlessly, but outside our chambers, we were just as compatible. Not seeing them on my left and right would be a rough adjustment.

Standing on the gravel drive in the moonlight, Tarn watched me stow my single carry bag. He's not ish-mikhan and not permitted to express melancholy. I read it in his face no matter how fiercely he hid it. Gilmore also held his tongue, pressing his lips together when our eyes met. These two were younger than me and if Master Pebb caught them pining, he would smash them on the spot. They both sent me a silent "kazak," and turned away, leaving me alone with the driver, awaiting my master's parting sentiments.

Finally, Elder Pebb emerged from the castle and held me in his arms several long moments before I boarded the carriage. I had long-ago memorized his scent and the feel of his amazing strength. An Elder isn't simply stronger—*utter power oozes from his pores*. I've inquired of my brethren if they discern this and none of them do. My proctor, Master Adonis, said this is an ish-mikhan trait; I will always see more in the Elders than the rest of our people. Moreover, he says that I see Elders the way the Fathers do, which is not only amazing, but also a heavy responsibility. As my master whispered in my ear how many times I had serviced him, promising he made a mental file of each of the twenty-thousand occasions, I recorded the moment. I would play it back a hundred thousand times over the course of my life. Still, he sent me away.

In the carriage ride that would take me from Pebb to Elder Emil (so he thought), I rode alone. I invited the higher-ranking soldier accompaniment to ride with me, but none accepted. I admit, I wondered why. They all like me (well, they all want to be on my good side). It was three evenings before the lieutenant explained.

"It's like this, ishy," he had said over a piss break the third night, "and you'll learn it, too, as they continue your military training…" Then he looked aside to his captain and they shared a chuckle. "How that's going to work, I don't know. *Shit!*" Then he returned to me with a stern gaze. "A soldier on duty needs his dick hard and his seed in. Anything else is unacceptable."

He wanted me to learn that Rakum soldiers do not orgasm on active duty, for this reason, the military compliment kept their distance to avoid involuntary arousal. I grinned at the thought, they had a right to worry. The lieutenant joined his men, leaving me alone until time to load up and move on. No problem, I made do, entertaining myself, by myself and *with* myself, always making plenty of noise. By the seventh night they grew accustomed to my presence and relaxed the quarantine. We played cards, drank, and ate together, developing camaraderie. One evening along the way, we stopped at a boisterous Italian pub for food and diversion.

Eleven of my brethren crammed into the small dining room, separated from the main patronage by coin and hypnotic suggestion. I had been winning at cards when the soldier on my right shared his tale of meeting Father Yuris.

Man by man, the stories went about the table. Every Rakum meets one of the Ten Fathers before he graduates

First Ritual, and for most of us, we will not see them again. At Assembly, they remain in their chamber and if we see a Father outside of the one event, it would be for the purpose of punishment. So, as I continued to win at poker and listen to my brothers, my own meeting with the Father came to mind.

Before I can tell you about that, however, you need to know why I might faint when first laying eyes on a Rakum Father. . .

3

Darcy, Don't Faint

IN HIS MEMOIR, JERSEY TOLD THE TALE of little Darcy seeing an Elder for the first time. Yes, I fainted. You have no idea what they look like to us (the ish-mikhan), so try not to judge. The average grunt views an Elder as a stronger, mightier, version of himself. And all of us detect Elders on sight because of the way they carry themselves. An ish-mikhan sees an aura around all Rakum. This halo around Elders glows brighter and can make us weak in the knees. Because I had not been prepared when I saw my first Elder, I hit the floor when our eyes met. It went like this.

Moldavia, 1719. My lair house had four proselytes, me being the oldest at age nine. I was much bigger than average, 5'11" by then, so my proctor pegged me as a soldier. He began my military training along with the

Ritual exercises every Rakum undergoes. Larp, my master, and his subordinate, a proctor-in-training named Cho-Now, pummeled me senseless every opportunity because I could endure it. I used it, too, excelling in hand-to-hand combat. It never occurred to me that I would ever be anything more than a fantastic soldier.

Enter Elder Pebb.

The story goes, he had a habit of collecting grunts he found intellectually or sexually interesting, so when he heard the Fathers wanted Larp's group lair investigated (they sensed something, I suppose), Pebb accepted the assignment. This Elder was tall and trim with broad shoulders and he arrived dressed like an aristocrat. Defying contemporary fashion, Pebb was clean-shaven, having trimmed his black locks above his ears which framed his high cheekbones and brought out his severe azure eyes.

I had never seen an Elder at this point and he arrived without warning. We were eating the evening meal when Master Larp commanded we line up in the meeting hall. As the oldest, I took the lead and the other three followed by order of age. When I rounded the pillar and viewed the Elder's profile, my legs wobbled. Had I stepped in a divot? I got into position, four abreast with my lair mates and then noted the master's shimmering aura. I couldn't breathe, so amazed I was by the light emanating from his center. I remember thinking, *"This is a brother, right? What is making that light?"*

25

Then Larp began speaking of the youths in his charge. My heartrate increased imagining that amazing being turning to look at my face. I began a mantra, repeating inside, "Master, do not turn. Do not turn. Do not turn…"

But Larp's hand lifted and gestured toward us.

My head swam and my mantra became, "He's going to see me! He's going to see me…"

Elder Pebb's face turned, and as I was first in line, he met my eye before the others.

Thunk!

Yes, you know it. Young Darcy passed out.

I admit it's funny now, but then, I'd been wowed to unconsciousness. The first voice I heard when I awoke was Master Larp saying, "How could we know?" My vision was firming up and I looked his way. He added, "that face, those eyes… I'm blind as shit!"

I wanted to see the Elder and I squeezed my eyes, forcing them to focus.

Cho-now said very close by, "Gah! I would have fucked him every night!"

I tuned them out as my field of vision populated with the most glorious face I had ever seen. I was lying across the master's lap so I thought I should right myself. He bade me be still and leaned close to press his lips to my forehead. When he pulled back and grinned, I loved him more than life itself.

"Kazak, Darcy Vandiver," Master Pebb said in an

incredible silky voice, his silvery-blue eyes mesmerizing me to the core. Somewhere in the back of my mind, I realized we sat in an unfamiliar room with a large bed, overloaded with body-size pillows. I didn't care about any of that, but I held my master's gaze, wishing with all of my heart to disappear inside of him, somehow become one with the amazing being who held me in his tender grip. Pebb grinned, reading my thoughts as easily as you might read the paper. He smiled wide and kissed my mouth.

"We are one already, little brother…"

Oh, shit, nine-year-old Darcy could have died that night and been happy to have lived just that one second. My master's telepathic voice, oh, I remember it even now—whispering across my psyche, I was home—*really* home.

"Now that I have found you, we will only grow closer."

And as it turned out, he was right. That very evening, Elder Pebb took me away from there, and that very night, I fixed my master for the first time.

Oh, I love that memory. Jersey wrote about it in great detail in his memoir *(Blood, Sex & Violence, A Vampire's Rebuttal),* but this is what I wanted to express for this particular book. I'm going to hold onto that memory of Elder Pebb's lips pressed to mine, his mental thread pulsating with light and life and everything an ish-mikhan could ever desire. So now you will understand

27

why I entitled this chapter, *Darcy, Don't Faint.*

In that small dining room of the boisterous pub, my brethren were swapping stories about meeting a Father for the first time. Think about it. If seeing an Elder can put an ish-mikhan's lights out, imagine what affect a Father might have!

The night I was to meet the Father, Master Pebb prepared me as best he could. He sat me down facing him, also seated, and stared into my eyes. He commanded me to see his memories of meeting Father Abroghia. This Father is thought to have spawned our race, and we all considered him the most powerful of all. The legend surrounding his name pegged him at more than three thousand years old, so I watched Master Pebb's recollection and was awed nearly to unconsciousness. He did this with me seven nights in a row leading up to the Father's arrival. When the night came, I steeled my nerve and stood ready facing the door.

I was seventeen and finished with the Ritual. Master Pebb assured me that I had done better than any grunt in his lifetime, which is a huge compliment. He told me as we awaited the Father's arrival that being ish-mikhan made many of my sort too weak to excel in the fierce trials all brethren complete. But I surprised him again and again by surpassing them all.

"You are king of the fuck and king of the Ritual—Father Damien will be proud."

Damien! It was the first time the identity was

revealed and my skin prickled. Damien was known to be High Father Abroghia's favorite companion. They were thought to actually enjoy each other's company, when as a rule, the Fathers enjoy nothing, as joviality is banal and useless to a god.

Master Pebb vanished then, zooming from my presence faster than my eye could follow. I heard the carriage in the courtyard and straightened my spine. I had memorized the protocol—he will open the door and see me, I stand at attention with my hands clasped behind my back, and then speak the script. With my eyes on the door, I visualized my success. Master Adonis taught me how to focus down so tightly that I did not think it possible that I would faint.

The door opened wide and as the form of the Father was several yards yet close, he had opened it with telekinesis. Father Damien's shape grew, filled the door, and he entered, dressed in black from head to toe, with a black hat and flowing cape.

I didn't faint or lose my tongue.

"Father Damien, I am honored to meet you," I said with the perfect inflection. "My will is your will. Please, let me serve you!"

I exclaimed the final word without intention, my pulse had ramped and even as I closed my mouth, I commanded my heart to resume the steady pace of rest.

Father Damien smiled, showing strong teeth, and he held out one hand. "Come close," he said and I all but clambered forward.

I was a couple inches taller, and he had me enter his space, standing at arm's length. He put both hands to my outer arms and stared into my face, his chin tilted up. My instincts sent me a command to hunker so I wouldn't be looking down upon my master.

"No," Damien commanded aloud and in my head. Then his eyebrows lifted and he grinned to the side. "You made a mistake there, didn't you?"

I was confounded; did he want me to admit I misjudged his needs? Was this a test? And wait… *did I* mis-read my master? I was not yet eighteen, but Master Adonis and Elder Pebb assured me I had excelled in all things. All this ran past my mind as I stared into Father Damien's hazel-green gaze. He held the same question in his expression, awaiting my reply. No matter what the consequence, my top priority was to be truthful. Deceit is never allowed between master and grunt.

"Father, I did not make a mistake," I said softly, transmitting with my eyes my adoration and worship. "When I drew close, subconsciously you preferred I lower myself."

I watched his eyes. If I was to be punished, I would welcome it. If I was to be praised, I would revel in that equally. All I wanted was for my master to be served. Then, as the seconds passed, Damien exhaled with a new grin and gave me a small nod. I parted my feet and we stood level.

"Pebb told me you were feisty," Damien said, a soft quality to his voice I hadn't expected. Then he formulated a new challenge, which I saw clearly in his thread. I wanted so badly to fulfill his will that I spoke before he did.

"Fight," I said low, answering before he asked, *what did I like to do most in the world.*

"Let me say my words, Darcy," he said kindly. "There is power in my words. Do you know this lesson?"

I shook my head, searching my memory. "Please, tell me about this power, Master."

He dropped the smile and lowered his eyes to his hands on my arms. As he slid the contact upwards to my throat, he watched the movement and only re-met my gaze when both warm palms encircled my neck.

"See what I see, Darcy Vandiver. See it now."

I hadn't had such a lesson, but following my instincts, I softened my will and waited. A thin gauze veiled my vision and I allowed it, consciously not clearing my mind. Through the haze, my master gave a nod.

"Words have substance and power. For this reason, your…"

I gasped as what appeared to be sound waves rippled across the veil, pulsing in cadence with the Father's phrases.

"…For this reason, your masters do not waste them. My words perform my will. Watch the table."

I averted my face inches to take in the nearby furniture, hazy through the film.

"Words destroy," he said, and several glass dishes shattered on the table surface.

My eyes grew wide in my surprise—we'd all seen telekinesis performed, but never did I realize words could cause it.

"Words create," he added and the flowers in the vase thickened and multiplied as I watched. "You speak. See your words," he said then and I gulped before giving it a try.

"You have taught me a wonderful new thing," I said and watched the ripples filter out and away, the ring effect stretched a dozen meters toward the far reaches of the room.

The Father abruptly dropped his hands and my vision snapped back to normal. He met my eyes and smiled—my face did that. He liked my face quite a lot and as I read that from his mind, he licked his lips and chuckled.

"My will is to watch you enjoy yourself," he said and turned me by a finger to my shoulder and we proceeded side by side. "And your favorite past time is roughhousing." He seemed amused at the information and added, "I am calling in my best soldier. Take us to your sparring room. I will watch you fight."

Now I grinned and picked up our pace, leading the Father down the first hallway to the cellar doors. His top guy—would he be huge? Could he be bigger than me? I was young, but larger than the Rakum I'd met so far.

Damien chuckled and had a word of advice. "Pullet will smash you, *unless…*" he said the word as a secret, "…unless you recall this new teaching."

Oh… I should use my words. How, I wasn't sure, but Father Damien wanted to see me enjoy myself. What would I enjoy most? Defeating a royal soldier before his eyes! Pleasing my master was my top priority, and in seventeen years, I had never failed. Poor Pullet... he was in trouble. Damien laughed at my thoughts and we entered the gym.

I hear some of you wondering why the Father did not seem interested in sex. This is because the Fathers do not fuck, they *breed.* When necessary, a Father can impregnate a breeder on the first try, but Fathers do not fuck other than on that occasion. Every Rakum understands to our deepest parts that the Fathers are divine. So when it comes to pleasing Father Damien, I only had to defeat Pullet in the ring.

The brethren had cleared the arena and I had a sense that they had exited the estate. As I said before, for most of us meeting a Father happened once, so the only Rakum I sensed around were those traveling with the entourage. One of these was Pullet and as I chose a spot to wait, I anticipated what he might look like. Father Damien stood to the side, his face turned toward me. I could no longer see his eyes, which had something to do with his mood. He had shrunk inside himself to witness the battle, but I did have a palpable sensation of his gaze on my flesh, as if the very action of *looking* had a weight and a measurable substance. It crawled along my arms jointly and moved toward my neck in perfect unison, encircled my throat, petted and stroked my chin. I'll end by saying the Father wanted to feel me with his eyes and he certainly did. I enjoyed his attention so much, that I did not notice when his best soldier entered.

"Father!" a loud voice boomed and I swiveled to face my opponent. "This ishy-fuck? Please! Let me fight a woman. A woman would be a mightier warrior than this… this… *courtesan!*"

I grinned when Pullet met my eye, his words could never offend me. Ish-mikhan are perfect in their way and I knew to my very atoms that this enormous brother simply enjoyed the sound of his own voice. He wanted to fuck me so badly, he could not imagine bruising me in war. His eye twitched in our gaze; all these things I read direct from his mind. And oh, how he hated that I knew his thoughts.

"Oh, yes, if Father Damien would only have mercy," Pullet said, not looking at our superior, still enjoying his own banter. Words were powerful, and Pullet wasted plenty already. When that thought crossed my mind, the Father's delicious gaze petted me again and I advanced.

Let me paint you a picture of this statuesque brute.

Pullet looked to be my height, but where I had barely filled out my teen-aged flesh, he'd packed a century of muscle and Rakum glory on his same-size skeleton. I would look like that in a few decades, a chest too wide to wrap my arms all the way around, a tapering muscled torso, bare since he entered shirtless and wearing only cotton trousers. I wanted to see it all, what would he look like in the buff? Don't laugh, but I wanted to see what Darcy Vandiver might have in his pants in a hundred years. I allowed him to see everything in my eye and because of my specialty, everything from my perspective had attached to it some element of sex.

"Are you ready, ishy-fuck? You do a lot of fawning, but the Father thinks you can fight. Come on," he assumed a stance and gestured with his fingers that I should come near.

I still had not uttered a word, looping the Father's instruction in my mind. *Words have power...* I took a couple of steps toward the man, holding his eye and showing him my beautiful smile. It affected him; I had already noted his erection tenting the cut of his pants but as I kept up my assault, his taunts grew softer and a smile found the side of his mouth.

"Judas Priest! I'm growing old here!" he barked, his eyes laughing. I only raised my brow and he shook his head. "I told the Father I would knock you unconscious, break you in many pieces, leave you for your Elder to heal in his quarters."

I released a small huff and rolled in my bottom lip, holding it with my teeth. When he lost his words a moment watching this maneuver, I zoomed forward with all of my might and collided, my shoulder lowered to crash into his solar plexus. He'd been surprised by the move and he knocked aside. I leapt free and circled around, resuming my stance.

"If you want to hug me, Ishy, just ask," he said matching my crouch and turning as I did. "Do it slower, though. I want to feel that silky hair in my fingers when I yank that shit out."

In his eye, I counted to three and then lifted to put both of my hands into my hair, running it through my fingers one cycle. Pullet watched without blinking, and his mind sent over a dozen fantasies that involved my hair in his lap.

Words are power...

Pullet had spoken so many words and he was no closer to winning the battle. I had a notion that if I said the right word, he and I would never come to blows. If I said the right word, he'd go to his knees and probably beg to suck me off.

His eyes grew and he laughed. "Fuck, Ishy! You are the most arrogant shit of all!" He moved toward me and lunged. I scooted away, a full miss.

The words came to me then and I peeked at the Father in my peripheral vision. His eyes were still unseeable, but he watched as before. If I said the words,

Pullet would concede the fight, I would win without lifting a finger. Is this what the Father desired? I didn't have to ask my muse—it gave me the notion in the first place. I had interpreted that the Father's desire was to see me fight Pullet with muscle. But my muse helped me see the truth of it—I would say the words. If delivered in the proper way, Pullet would drop his notion for fisticuffs altogether.

I wanted to fight, to feel my fists connect with Pullet's hard flesh and smell his sweat and exertion as he wrestled a lesser brother until one of us cried uncle. But tonight was about Father Damien; he had taught me a new lesson and wanted an exhibition of that teaching. This is what would fix him; I would make him smile. It was time.

Pullet sensed I was up to something and he raised inches from his stance, his handsome face shining with expectation, his bright green eyes full of violence and passion. I parted my lips to speak and he stopped breathing, listening, wondering…

I bided my time. The seconds passed. Two, three, four…

His sideways smile widened.

Five, six, seven…

He wanted to hurry me up, force me to speak, but he held his peace, watching my mouth. And then, I inhaled, filling my lungs and when I released the air, I pushed words from my mouth, vowels and consonants that flowed as if three-dimensional, sounding like, *"Master, you are magnificent. If you were to go to your knees, I'd beg you to take me right here, right now. I need you. Please."*

Pullet dropped to his knees between the words, "right" and "now." *Thunk.* He was down, his huge arms lowered, his shoulders rounding, and he sat back on his heels and looked at me in wonder.

The battle had ended.

To my right, Father Damien nodded and sent me a kazak as he faded from sight. I looked at Pullet and stepped into his space. As he was, he looked up at me when I came close enough to touch.

"I've never had an ish-mikhan," he whispered and opened his hands for me to enter his embrace.

He hugged me at first like a mortal, tender, both arms folding me to his body. I returned the move, my right hand stroking his sweaty locks. Then, he remembered who he was—a royal lieutenant, Father Damien's top soldier and traveling companion—and he began the job of removing my clothing. He had never stood so close to a fix-it man and he took his time examining me. When I showed him all I felt he needed, he was happy. And I was, too. I saw the future Darcy and he was goddamn beautiful.

Every.

Single.

Inch.

4

An Extraordinary Gift

WHEN I WAS A YOUNG SEVENTY (I am 310 at the penning of this memoir), my master decided to send me to another Elder to continue my training. Let me tell you how that night went. It contains blood, sex, and violence, which you know by now are a Rakum's three favorite things.

My new master, Elder Kilmeade, had me ride with him in the carriage, zooming across the land toward his palatial Sicilian estate. We had been together several evenings, and he quite enjoyed my talents in the bedroom. This night, we found ourselves hungry for blood and stopped off at a local farmer's home where he offered travelers food for coin. My master stepped from the carriage first and I followed, positioning myself just behind his right shoulder because his top lieutenant took the left. I didn't approve of the soldier's avoidance of my eye. Kilmeade's military accompaniment should have fawned over the ish-mikhan in their midst, but none did.[6]

"Ignore them," Master Kilmeade sent to my mind with a mischievous wink. *"You belong to me and I do not share. They are safer pretending you disgust them, but they jerk off every sunup picturing your face."* With surprising levity, Kilmeade mimed the movement at his crotch and then pinched my ass. My previous Elder had been much more stoic, and I enjoyed the new master's lighthearted demeanor.

A few yards away, the farmer opened his front door to welcome us inside. He strolled into the night, meeting us halfway down the grassy path. At his command, three lads less than fifteen jogged from behind the cottage to care for our company's horses. Once the farmer introduced himself as Pavinni, Kilmeade and I entered. The lieutenant remained on the walk outside and before I could ponder it further, Kilmeade sent to my mind, *"I can't have that disgusting turd beside me amongst these mortals. Darcy Vandiver is all I need tonight."*

He was correct. I returned a cheery wink and we settled at a table where the farmer directed. I discerned females in the place and when they glided in to serve wine and anti-pasta, Kilmeade and I looked them over.

---

[6] Part of this was described in *Blood, Sex, and Violence a Vampire's Rebuttal,* but here is told from my perspective; it varies to some degree from Jersey's telling.

Rakum enjoy fucking females, but more than that, we enjoy drinking "freely offered blood." When a female consents her blood, it changes the flavor, turning it into the food of the gods. When my master and I eyed these three, we sized them up for both. I convinced Kilmeade that my ish-mikhan training would enable me to get all three of the women to consent. My master sent Pavinni to the barn (where we knew our brothers would drink and end him, as they already had the three boys) and told me to do my thing. The woman and her daughters were helpless in my gaze and I swooned them with barely any effort. My master grinned at my prowess and sent a new thought. *"Polcz-v*[7], *who will it be?"*

The girls were young, healthy, and well-formed and the woman still attractive at thirty. The women stood before us as if ready to serve more wine, looking aside when I caught their eyes. I replied to my master, *"I will drink the mother but bow to your will for the rest."*

Kilmeade read me very well and gave me a kind wink. *"You prefer to fuck your brothers,"* he sent and added, *"I have a wonderful surprise for you. You will not believe your eyes..."*

I wanted so much to know what he meant, for his context had me stiffening on the spot. But first, we needed blood.

Kilmeade took the teenager to a side room and I

---

[7] "Favored one," an ish-mikhan's favorite word in an Elder's mouth.

followed the mother to her bedchamber, leaving the youngest child alone in the dining area.

"What can I get for you, honorable sir?" the woman asked in Italian after securing the door's drop-lock.

"I hunger for your blood," I whispered, cradling her face in my hands, all the while hypnotizing her with my gaze.

Without reservation, she delivered over her will. I pulled free my small blade (Rakum do not have fangs; forget the idiotic movies. *We are real…*) and in a practiced movement the wound was made. I am 6'6", so I lifted her off the ground as I drank from her throat. When I had consumed my fill, I healed her wound with my palm and left her unconscious on the lumpy straw mattress. Feeling sublime and rubbing my middle, I came around the wall to find Kilmeade finished with the teen. He'd been brutal, which was his prerogative, but she would live. When our eyes met, I wondered again at the surprise he promised.

"Come, let us get underway. I long to see your face at this amazing gift."

I could barely contain my excitement, my body buzzing with the consented blood and my mind racing over the sexual gift my master had in mind.

In the carriage once more, the horses picked up their speed on the straightaways and my master was quiet, looking out the window to the night. I couldn't see his thoughts; as an Elder, he cloaked them, even from me, and my telepathy was superior. The teen's aroma clung to his skin and my mind wandered to his preferences. Maybe he enjoyed her more, maybe I wasn't enough. This train of thought brought a frown to his lips and he swiveled his face to mine.

"A mortal…" he began in our language and then fell into telepathy to finish. *"…a mortal is beneath me, beneath you. Beneath every brother in our population. I loathe them. I see them as dirty, roach-like, and simple-minded. But…"*

He paused and summoned me closer with two fingers. I dropped to the carriage floor to my knees and watched his face.

"Like a roach, they are useful. They maintain our planet," he said, switching now to Italian. "Both sexes have hands to work and soft places to release our lust. I will always prefer my kind over them. As you age, you will find no Rakum truly favors a human. Mark my word."

Master Kilmeade's words eased my worry and I remained on the floorboard looking up until very shortly, he grinned and invited me all the way in. That wench wasn't near enough for my master and I finished what she could not.

Hours later, we reached my master's estate.

"Oh, my precious pet!" he said with glee. "It is nearly time," he said, a twinkle of mischief in his bright gray eyes. "I have another *ish-mikhan*."

You should have seen my face at his admission. I had never met another fix-it man, but considering how amazing I was in my own mind, how much more so would I enjoy someone like me? I couldn't even imagine how wonderful he would be.

Kilmeade added, "His name is Jersey. It is my will that the two of you will be companions. You will be compatible and ply your skills together. This experiment will be my top priority until I am satisfied I have learned all I can."

The joy in Kilmeade's face at what he expected could not match my excitement. I attempted to peek into Kilmeade's mind to see my ish-mikhan brother, but he shook his head. The carriage had parked at the house entrance. I stepped down and Kilmeade followed and touched my elbow.

"Stand here. I must see your faces at the meet. Close your eyes; Pluto will lead you forward when I call."

I did as he commanded, my heart hammering. I absorbed the sounds of the brethren nearby, their body scents, and that of the livestock and a hearty stew cooking in the house. When Pluto took my bicep in hand and tugged forward, I stepped from gravel to smooth stone, gruffly led by the arm. Then, a new scent reached my nostrils; it was the ish-mikhan! He smelled of lavender soap and something close to my own aroma, pheromones and excited perspiration. I waited for the command to open my eyes. We were placed barely three feet apart; I felt the man's body heat and the sound of my heart obliterated all else.

Master Kilmeade said in my mind, *"Open your eyes."* Then aloud, "Darcy Vandiver, meet Jersey."

Oh… My inhale had been audible. This Rakum, holy shit!

The ish-mikhan named Jersey stepped close, craning his neck in an exaggerated movement, grinning wide at our height difference. I looked down on him, the most beautiful man I had ever seen—green eyes, emerald and shining, hair soft, wavy, and nearly the same color as my own, a strong build of balance and allure. It seemed much more than I deserved and as the thought tickled my inner mind, Jersey's eye twinkled. He lifted warm palms to either side of my face, diving deep into my gaze. I remained immobile, seeing in Jersey a future brighter than the sun.

"He's a romantic, Master," Jersey said gazing into my eyes. "He is magnificent."

Still speechless, I moistened my lips.

"You are home," Jersey sent, reading me more easily than any grunt ever had. Then Jersey applied the tiniest bit of pressure to my cheeks in case I wanted to lean down. *"Ish-mikhan don't need words, do we?"*

I lowered to his height, my head rushing with all I experienced.

"It is our master's will that we be compatible," Jersey said in a soft voice that flowed with substance to my ears. "Do you think we can do that?"

In drawing me into the house, Pluto had led me to a bedroom. With my head and groin pounding with blood, I cupped Jersey's neck with one hand and pulled him close. At first, I smashed our lips together, closed-mouthed and sealed tight. One, two, three seconds I held Jersey fiercely to my face. Then, when I relaxed the pressure to his neck, the kiss opened and I dove in, tasting him, withholding nothing.

Jersey chuckled, still connected, his breath filling my cheeks. I recognized the sound—it was joy. I felt it, too. Our embrace morphed into explorations, the difference in our heights no challenge as my right hand caressed Jersey's chest and at my middle, Jersey worked my belt.

I ripped my mouth away with a smack, my huge idiotic grin reflected in Jersey's shining face. With a violent shove, I pushed him onto the bed and hopped upon him in a straddle as our audience melted away. I propped my weight upon open hands at either side of Jersey's head to gaze into his face.

"What will you teach me, Master?" I sent to his mind, his seniority demarcated by chronological age, coupled with his training as ish-mikhan under the great Elder Kilmeade.

"Wonderful things," Jersey returned, our eyes locked, his knees coming up to my lower back. *"So many wonderful things."*

With another joyful chuckle from us both, Kilmeade's two ish-mikhan found ourselves more compatible than we could ever have imagined. And to this day, as you will read in this book and others in the series, Jersey remains my most compatible brother of 100,000. And goddammit, is he perfect in every way.

5

Hester, the Boil on My Ass

THIS PHOTO MAKES ME CHUCKLE. Last summer, Jersey was finishing up his memoir and he asked Hester to send in a picture of himself for the book inside matter.  This is what he sent. Don't get me wrong; it's perfect. It represents the man in every way. It makes me grin because of what a gigantic asshole brother Hester is. What makes him more asshole-ish than the rest of my brothers, you wonder? Well, I'll tell you.

Hester was younger by decades, coming into the world in 1814, born when the breeders were housed underground in upstate New York. The reason I mention the location is because twenty years later, four Rakum breeders died in a fire that this little shit started. Before 11/13[8], only our leaders were aware that he caused the destruction that horrid night.

The New Year had come and gone, 1955 promised to be a beautiful time for all of us living in the United States of America during this nation's growth and maturity. Hester lived where he'd been born, assigned to service the brethren that ran the facility. The Fathers had four living ish-mikhan to spread out (haha) in those days: Jersey, Hester, Julio, and myself. In February, my travels took me close enough to Portland, New York, that I swung in to check on their status. I would bring reports to my Elder who would share it with our Fathers. Plus, I knew Hester was there and I hadn't fucked him. Ish-mikhan are sometimes very compatible, such as with me and Jersey. I wanted to see if Hester would be a new favorite.

Let me describe the New York breeders' den (they vary in small degrees, but most are like this—simple and practical). From the outside, it looks like a large log cabin, its foundation T-shaped. Once you entered, the floorspace was sparse, the eye traveling to a door in the floor that they kept covered with a woolen mat. Once

---

[8] This is what we call the night we all turned mortal outside of our control. It was horrible. This night is chronicled in *Anomaly, Book Four of the Rabbit Saga* by Ellen C. Maze, Little Roni Publishers, LLC 2018.

you're in the house and the door is bolted behind you, that trap door will unlock and you can climb down. Our brothers are amazing builders, and along with that, excellent tunnelers. All over the globe, we have tunneled out thousands of miles of living spaces for traveling and stationary brethren. This den had three levels underground, meaning our engineers had set it atop natural caverns a century ago when it was chosen. Like I said, our workforce is amazing.

What is a breeder? It is a woman the Fathers impregnated with a new Rakum. Of the brethren, only the Ten Fathers were fertile, this meant none of us would ever get a woman pregnant. This is genius and I always thought so. The Fathers only had sex when it was time to breed a new brother, which only happened when our numbers fell off the 100,000-count that Father Abroghia assigned from the beginning of time.

Allow me to add that the breeders are volunteers, agreeing to be kept underground once they enter the program. Why would a female do this? Ask someone else; many humans over the centuries have given us blood and sex without expecting repayment. I believe they are insane, but it is what it is. Although we are not concerned with the breeders' "happiness," their health is directly related to the health of the coming brother. For this reason, they are well fed and have books, material pleasures, and access to each other at their whim.

When we arrived, I left my escorts to tend the

horses and I entered the den. The scent of females hung in the air and when I opened the trap door, their aroma filled my head with its particular sweetness. Humans might not know this, but when I say the aroma was sweet, it means it gave me pleasure. Drinking from *consenting* females was every Rakum's favorite fantasy because it was the most rare blood we could find. Well, not as rare as a Rakum Rabbit, but that's another book in itself.[9]

I climbed down the ladder into the dark tunnel lit only by muslin torches stationed every twenty feet. I detected four distinct women's body scents and then a few brethren, and more than one male mortal, probably Cows. As I followed my nose, I attempted to pick out Hester's signature. Ish-mikhan smell pretty—as my master once told me—and I made it all the way to the end of the current tunnel before I detected what might be lavender mixed with the day's perspiration. I stopped at a closed door and it opened inward, a brother bustling out and speaking to whomever was inside.

"I'll go see," he was saying as he slammed into my chest. "Shit!" he hissed and looked up as I was much taller. "Where'd you come from?" he asked in our language.

"Poulus S'ster?" (where is Hester) I asked and allowed my eyes to roam his face. He stepped back from

---

[9] *"Rabbit: Chasing Beth Rider* by Ellen C Maze revealed our race. Before that, we lived beneath your radar." ~ Darcy

the collision enough that we both looked each other over.

"Hester, somebody sent you a present," he said meeting my eye and calling to the dark room he'd been exiting. "Name's Petrov," he said to me using a soft new voice. "Can I stay? I'd give my left nut to see what you and that ishy-fuck are going to do together."[10]

I grinned by reflex at his words. This brother was my age and devastatingly handsome—dark hair and eyes, his skin shades darker than mine and I'm fairly swarthy for a Rakum.

"Do you like to fuck ish-mikhan, Petrov?" I asked to tease and he grinned to the side with a nod. "I'm off-duty. Will you fix me instead?" I had to ask, not opposed to sitting back when allowed.

"I will fix you until you pass out. What's your name?"

"Darcy Vandiver," I said and Petrov grinned.

"Darcy Vandiver—I will sing your name for the balance of my days."

Oh, I loved this one and he enjoyed my responding wide grin. He moved aside with flourish so I could enter the room.

"Hester's in the shitter," he said with a chuckle. "I fixed him just now. I'm always fixing that asshole, he's very cruel to ol' Petrov."

---

[10] *"Oh, the beauty of a Saga Collection! Later in life, Petrov played an enormous role in the shit of 11/13. Read about that in Anomaly, Beyond the Rabbit, by Ellen C Maze"* ~ Darcy

I walked in and heard another man in the next room, presumably Hester.

"You'll be nicer to me. You're a soldier; you know how hard we get on the campaign trail. I've been on the road two years and when I got assigned here, this fix-it man makes me work for the tiniest bit of attention." Petrov huffed. "Are you here to replace him?"

I laughed. "No, and Petrov," I said in a gentle tone, "Come here."

He stepped close, looking up at me, and even though he was strong and sexy, his expression made him look all of ten years old.

"Hester is fixing you," I said, all the while allowing my eyes to caress his psyche and I touched his cheek before cupping his throat with one hand.

"What do you mean?" he asked in a whisper, lost in my eyes or my voice or both.

"Does he fuck the other brothers differently?" I asked and Petrov nodded. "Hester is fixing them, too. The ish-mikhan has a living spirit inside who tells him what his master—or brother—wants. I call mine my muse. Hester's muse assured him that you need to work for your pleasure."

"That's crazy," he replied, no anger in his tone.

"Let's ask my muse right now how to fix Petrov." I lifted my second hand and held his face looking deep into his eyes. "What do you want?" I asked.

In less than an instant, Petrov's subconscious sent

an image of him on his knees, his arms hugging my waist. He read some of this in my eyes and shook his head.

"I want you doing that to me," he whispered.

"Sorry, lover, but my muse is never wrong." I kissed his mouth and walked past. Hester was coming out and I wanted to meet him with a clear mind.

"Petrov's blood pressure is turning me deaf," the ish-mikhan said as he joined us. He sought my gaze and then to my amazement, Hester pointed his finger to my face and said, "You're too big and hairy to win a spot in my bed."

Petrov's face flicked between us, no doubt as surprised as I was. The redhead's words were an obvious provocation, but at the same time, I was certain he wasn't interested in fighting. Internally choosing my words, I held my tongue as the shit stepped closer.

"Show me your magic wand," he said then, his eyes dropping to my trousers. "Can I count on that, at least, being perfect?"

His insults astounded me, and I had no reply. I certainly could not say any of these idiotic phrases about Hester. He was *beautiful*. Angular and chiseled facial features, emerald green eyes even more dramatic than Jersey's, with a tight and athletic build standing right at six feet. Here was a man without flaw or blemish. Why did he feel compelled to punish my pride?

I hadn't yet spoken and he stood under my nose. I

54

held my face static and my muse had fallen quiet. Hester's fingers went to my middle and he shoved a hand down the front of my still-fastened jeans. His eyes went soft and thoughtful as he mapped my manhood with skilled fingers. I wanted to laugh.

I asked inside, *"What is going on here?"*

"Watch and see..." I heard deep in my inward parts.

"Hester, what are you saying?" Petrov asked in wonder. "This is the most magnificent man I have ever seen."

"Leave us," Hester said, and the soldier did as instructed, probably because he wanted to remain on the fix-it man's good side. Hester withdrew his hand and remained close. "I don't like you."

Ahh. I got it.

I told you earlier—ish-mikhan are more human than ordinary grunts. We suffer some of the emotions you guys have and our brethren allow it because of the payoff in bed. My mouth tucked into a half-grin my eyes in Hester's. The brother was *jealous.* Can you believe it? As if we were in competition!

"It's too crowded here for you," he continued but didn't step back. "I'll let you jerk me off, but then I want you to leave."

I chuckled. I wasn't going anywhere near his shit; surely he knew it. He liked the sound of his own voice.

Voice...

He hadn't heard mine and it was my superpower. I decided at that moment that I would accept the gauntlet Hester threw down. I would engage him in a battle of wills and my victory would be this lovely red-haired ishy begging me to fuck his brains out. *Let the games begin!* I said to my muse and Hester's eyes widened as if he sensed it.

"What are you up to?" he asked and backed one step. "I am telling you the truth; I don't like you. You're not my type. I'm not even the slightest bit interested in you."

Oh, he was in trouble. I had devised a plan of attack and he was still yammering on. Telepathically, I called for Petrov who poked his head in as if he'd been waiting for it. *"Bring me some rope,"* I sent to his mind and the man disappeared.

Hester sought an answer, his ethereal fingers prodding my mind. I allowed him to see himself tied to a sturdy chair. Hester turned as if to bolt away. No matter what he thought of me sexually, he correctly discerned that I outclassed him in sheer physicality. I surged into position and grabbed him from behind, my arms about his chest.

"Shhhh," I cooed in his ear, holding him just tightly enough that I did not fracture his ribs. He squirmed and complained and Petrov jogged in, a nice length of hemp in hand. I dragged Hester to a fat-legged oak chair and forced him to sit. *"Bind him up,"* I sent to

56

the soldier's mind, holding my audible words for the correct timing.

Grinning with the game, Petrov did as requested, double, triple, and quadruple tying Hester's legs to the chair and then about his waist and chest to the back. Hester's curses rang throughout the room, echoing with the power of his effort and I had Petrov shove a pocket cloth into his open mouth.

"There," I said in my silkiest tone, circling around for Hester to see me. His handsome face turned upward, beads of perspiration reflecting the light of the torches.

"I don't like you," he sent to my mind, the words muffled into his gag.

But he did. He liked Darcy Vandiver. He liked my long body, my tawny skin, my yellow-gold irises. He liked the way my mouth moved, how my tongue wet my lips and withdrew, how my silky brown hair fell across my shoulders when I leaned down.

I opened my stance, chose a good spot, and sat on his lap facing him, straddling him as he was tied well to the furniture. His eyes petted my sculpted shoulders, my biceps and then my chest muscle as it pressed into my shirt. His erection tented his slacks no matter how he pretended it did not.

"You ugly motherfucker! Get off me!" he shouted in my mind.

The battle of wills was underway, but I had a secret weapon. Hester did not notice how carefully I had been keeping my words few. His beautiful eyes held mine, his struggling lessening moment by moment. I took my time and rolled up the sleeves of my dress shirt, and Hester watched, his brow knitting with interest at the shape of my forearms. These were arms that could embrace him, cuddle him close, press him bodily into my hard flesh. Hester no longer struggled, having grown quiet. I pulled out the cloth and he moistened his palate, his eyes in mine.

"I don't…" he began and stopped.

It was time for me to use my voice and I settled my weight a little more, my buttocks against his thighs.

"Hester, so beautiful and perfect, you could know the pleasure of fucking Darcy Vandiver—you could feel my weight draped over you, my matchless stroke bringing an ecstasy you can't even imagine…"

My voice had the man in pieces. It didn't matter if he was ish-mikhan; at this moment, Hester had lost all will of his own.

"Tell me what you want, baby doll," I cooed, allowing one palm to caress his cheek and then rest at his throat. My hand is so large I could stroke his chin with my thumb and cup the back with my four fingers. He felt my size on him and he looked lost.

"I don't…" he said and stopped again.

"Tell me, baby, I need to hear it," I whispered and leaned in to press my lips to his forehead. The tilt of my hips caused our clothed erections to make contact and he inhaled as I sat up again. I was about to win. His will dissolved. He had to say the words… *"Say it, lover. Say it now,"* I sent to his mind, my lips parted.

Hester gave up the battle, conceding to the more experienced fix-it man. "Fuck," he sighed, his eyes in mine, as soft and alluring as the most expensive whore. "Whatever I have is yours," he said in a little-boy voice. "Please let me fix you, Master. Please…" he begged.

I smiled, pecked his sweaty forehead again, and stood.

"Petrov!" I called in a loud voice and the man ran to my side from nearby as before. "Take me to your bed, brother. Hester will listen from here."

"What?" Hester rasped.

As his master, I commanded him to wait just like that, assuring that someone would release him before sunup.

"Master? Darcy? Wait…"

With a victorious grin, I followed Petrov across the floor. And trust me, I made sure to have the noisiest sex of my life. I forced Hester to sit there and take it. Of all the nerve. My appearance is perfect. Hester sealed his fate the moment he spoke against my beauty. He should have known better.

And goddamn, was Petrov thankful.

6

Tole: Sexy & Tragic

Part I: Tole, the Horrible Lover

*Photo Caption: This looks very much like this beautiful
brother, so let us pretend it's him… ~ Darcy*

RAKUM CAN LIVE HUNDREDS OF YEARS, even
millennia if we're smart. That said, very few of us live to
be six hundred years old. I can think of two Elders who
surpassed that mark, and of course the Fathers each had
seen two thousand years minimum, but for the grunts, in

1965, I was one of the older ones, especially in my circles.

My circles. About that.

In 1965, I traveled with Master Bel off and on and sometimes Jack Dawn. These two Elders were huge, taller and heavier than I was by far, and they loved to get me into the ring. Bel still fucked me now and then, but at 1200 years old, Jack hadn't screwed anyone for centuries. By the time Tole entered my timeline, both masters had moved onto fresh flesh, so I sought a companion to keep myself sharp. I had hoped it would be this alluring brother.

Tole. Tole. Tole.

Tole was practically my height, although if they put a stick to it, I'd be a hair taller. But our fantastic physiques were a remarkable match. The hilarious thing about Tole was his appearance alone set me on fire, but as it turned out, he was horrible in bed. But that's Tole. Right now, I'm imagining him; why am I hard? Wait. I haven't finished telling you.

Let me slow down.

Master Bel called me to him one night and I barely met his eye before I heard his will—he wanted me to go away. Elder Bel's subconscious sent, *"I want to not look at you for a month."* You might think I'd be disheartened, but that's not the way it works with my kind. We seek our master's will, so fulfilling his request made me happy. With a bow, I turned and left the room.

I gathered a carry sack, a pubescent grunt who had already been assigned as my valet, and left Bel's estate.

"Where are we headed, Master?" Bekan asked as we piled into a mortal taxicab.

I didn't answer but gave the driver the address. It was a waystation on the outskirts of town where I could find brothers and maybe figure out a place to land until my master once again longed to see my face and feel my touch.

Bekan didn't ask again and I ruffled his hair. He was small, but only twenty at this time (he would grow into a great looking brother with light brown hair to his mid-back and the bluest eyes you've ever seen), would have looked fifteen to mortals, gangly and awkward, with too-long limbs and a perpetually worried expression.

I laugh at the memory, but because sometimes he was the only one around, I taught him how to give head. He was awful, just so clumsy, as if he didn't have a dick himself. But it's not his fault; he wasn't mature yet, had never had an intuitive hard-on, and anyway, he wasn't ish-mikhan. I give all of them a little grace because of that.

Halfway through the ride, I busted the driver, stealing long glances at me in the rearview mirror. Mortals don't have to be Cows to find us appealing, and me being ish-mikhan made it even more difficult to hide their attraction. I allowed him three more quick looks and finally scooted up so I'd speak at his ear from behind.

"You can blow me if you like, but I'm not fucking you."

The cabbie gasped, his eyes darted to the mirror, to the road, and then he jerked his chin to the right to see if he craned his face a little, he might look at me directly.

"Pull over before you wreck," I whispered, allowing my magical voice to pet him all over.

"Fuck, fuck, fuck," he mumbled, maneuvering the car across lanes despite angry honks of other drivers. He hissed a few more fucks and turned onto an off-street, rolling to the end of the block and parked against the curb. He shoved the gearshift to park and dropped his hands, palm open to both thighs.

"What? What did you say?" he whispered.

"Do you want to blow me?" I asked him in my bedroom voice and he nodded like a child, still regarding me in the reflection in the rearview. "Trade places with Bekan." I leaned back and the cabbie scrambled out of the car. My little ward also got out and they swapped, Bekan behind the wheel and the cabbie sitting by my side.

"You smell pretty good," I told him and allowed my gaze to stroke him, beginning at his stormy blue eyes to his open mouth, full lips moistened, quivering, to his throat—I'd probably let Bekan drink him tonight—and I grinned at his strong chest and spreading middle.

"Lift your shirt," I told him and he did without delay. Rakum are hard, incapable of storing adipose, so it's no wonder we enjoy touching mortals, soft and warm in all the right places. His belly was furry, I liked that, too and I would have touched it if he was a Cow. But he was just a horny man turned on by my natural magnetism. So I told him to stroke his own belly.

"Pet it like it's a big scary cat," I said and he loved me with his whole heart when I smiled in his eyes. He ran one palm across his middle and then again and again, his gaze on my face and my attention to his fuzzy middle. It was enough, I was ready. "You want to suck my cock, Cabbie?"

"Yes, yes, I do, I will," he stammered and I realized he didn't sleep with guys much. I gave him a little nod and he moved closer, carefully opening my belt and fly enough. I made him work for it, barely helping. Then I watched him do his very best to make me smile.

"I want you to drink this guy when he's done," I sent Bekan who had swiveled from the front seat to watch. *"Oh, now look, you could learn this—see what he's adding there?"* I smiled and we both watched the driver do a bang-up job for a mostly straight guy. I closed my eyes for the ending and the fucker surprised me and swallowed. As worthless as Bekan can be, he was in the backseat with us as the driver was sitting up. I was able to lean back and enjoy the glow as Bekan took the man's blood with little complaint.

We were less than a block from the address so we left him there, groggy and confused, and struck out on foot. We felt sublime. Time to find our brothers—as you've discovered, at this point, I much preferred them over mortals. I figured someone at the waystation would be a decent lay and I was right. It wouldn't be Tole, but let's get back to his story.

The corner building we sought and located boasted a sign in English, "Tax Preparation CLOSED TIL SPRING." Underneath in our language were two symbols for "waystation," which the mortals would think were runes or sigils. Bekan followed me to the doors, I opened the lock with telekinesis, and we slipped inside.

I would describe the aroma in this closed-up safe-space as soil mixed with sweat and rusted iron pipe. I didn't smell my brethren and this had me curious. I didn't need light to see and we proceeded to the furthest corner of the cavernous unfurnished floorspace. I reached a closed door and pushed it open. When Bekan and I were through, I allowed it to close and lock. Still no brethren. No heart-sounds, no body aroma.

Bekan's telepathy was shitty, but he was able to send a question mark sentiment and I bade him be patient. I found the cellar steps and descended, still without light, and this deep into the house, he and I were using our other senses since even Rakum eyes do not see in absolute dark.

Then I heard them. Two of our brethren entwined in some sort of quiet physical amusement. Using only my ears, it sounded decidedly unpleasurable. Had we come upon some sort of punishment fuck? I chuckled at the thought and one of the brothers inside noticed, instructing in an authoritative tone that we should identify ourselves.

I gave the proper response in our language. "Darcy Vandiver and Bekan, Elder Bel's pack."

A flashlight beam speared Bekan's face and he covered his eyes. I walked toward the source and the beam searched my chest and then down to my toes before a lamp came on.

"Fuck me," the torchbearer said. This guy was nude, sitting sideways on an ancient brown couch, and yes, he was beautiful. Black hair, loose curls kept just long enough to fist in my hands. A heart-shaped face, its sexiness accentuated with a trimmed beard. His hazel-green eyes met mine and I wanted him so bad, right then right there. I can tell you in all honesty that in the moment, I knew I'd be fucking him off and on my entire life (and I have until only recently).

But this wasn't Tole. Don't fret, I'm getting there.

The nude brother dropped the flashlight to the couch to stand and came close. *"Dars-s-s-s,* eh?" he said dragging the *s*, "Name's Pitch."

I must have had my lovestruck-stupid-asshole-face on because the shit grinned and closed the distance without asking permission. He reached up, cupped my cheeks, requesting I lower to his height. He pressed our mouths together and I did not object, our chemistry undeniable. The other guy, who I would learn was named Tole, could be heard nearby but out of sight. Pitch was kissing me, sucking my tongue and his strong fingers were digging at my belt.

"Fucking fix-it man," Pitch whispered in my mind, his silent voice even sexier than I expected. *"I will fix you first, asshole. Just watch…"*

"Fuck-yeah, go for it," I returned and relinquished the last of any question of how to proceed. I allowed Pitch to lead the dance and in another two minutes, he pinned me to the tattered sofa. We were in deep when Tole approached Bekan. I only attended enough to know the brother was also naked and sought satisfaction from my ward he hadn't received from Pitch. Because this isn't *that kind of book,* let me sum-up: Pitch fixed me, wholly, entirely, throwing every ounce of effort into his performance, and when we traded position, he knew precisely how to keep the ardor alive until we'd both met an amazing end—me twice. Finally, exhausted and smiling like idiots, he hugged up against me under my arm and we watched Bekan fail at getting poor Tole off.

"This is the funniest shit I've ever seen," Pitch said with a knuckle to the youth. "This *peiltz[11]* lives with the sexiest Rakum on the continent and this is how he delivers pleasure?"

---

[11] Rakum Hungarian for "shitter," a worthless person.

Standing ten feet away and watching Bekan do his thing, Tole swiveled his face to ours, the first time I'd seen his bright blue eyes and he said to me, "Pitch always has the best luck. He gets the prince and I end up with a floundering puppy."

"Don't give up, Beek," I said, holding Tole's gaze. Then I grinned and his face softened. "That's an order."

"Judas Priest," he said in a grunt, having fully heard my voice for the first time. It's deep and throaty; Jersey said some of the brothers come just from hearing it. Tole rolled his hand in my direction. "Please, brother, say something else. Oh, shit, I almost had it. That voice..."

I gave him a new grin and held his eye with tenacity. "Tole, you want to hear my voice, but you're so stove up that if I speak, you might injure my valet with the power of your..."

That was all he required; Bekan was shoved hard to the cement floor in Tole's explosion of pleasure. Pitch laughed uproariously and when I saw the boy was knocked out but alive, I reached for my discarded jeans. By the time the three of us were dressed and making small talk about current Rakum events, Bekan sat up, rubbed the back of his healed cranial fracture and wobbled over to our position.

"Elder Bel set you loose?" Pitch confirmed and I nodded. "You're bunking with me." He had turned a threatening glare to Tole as he spoke and Tole's eyes darkened with sudden fury.

"The hell he is!" Tole said and surged close, chest out, facing down Pitch with a growl.

Tole outweighed Pitch by fifty pounds and like me, stood a good four inches taller. A fight might be fun so I asked if they had a match room. My brothers spat curses at each other as we crossed to the next room. Clear of any furniture, they immediately dropped into their stance, both ripping off the shirts we had all just re-donned. Then, it was on. Pitch and Tole slapped together, embracing in an evil wrestling hug, neither giving in for several long seconds. Pitch was a captain, I saw this plainly in his behavior and now that I watched them fight, his technique said the same. Tole fought like a flower girl. He was larger and stronger, but his technique sucked. I watched them switch tactics from wrestling to boxing and Pitch landed many more blows.

In another few minutes, Tole looked to be wearing down. He flashed me a quick look before Pitch clocked his jaw hard enough that his eyes glazed. Aw, shit, I don't know why, but I yanked off my shirt, tossed it over Bekan's head, and dove in between my two brethren. In my crouch I waited for Pitch to attack me as he had our weaker brother.

"You haven't had enough of Pitch, eh?" he whispered, circling and watching for his moment. "How about I force-fuck you when I get you down? You're a mountain, but I suspect…"

He talked too much.

In a blur, I zoomed into his space, my right hook fracturing his jaw with its power. Pitch's brain must have sloshed a little too much because he went down and didn't get up. I stood over him a moment, listening to his heart and measuring his blood pressure, and Tole came up behind me to land both hands to my shoulders.

"You're a captain, too," he said, his voice soft. I turned and we stood eye to eye. "Kazak," he said even lower and I read an attractive adoration in his gaze most brethren hid.

Have you ever looked into another person's eyes long enough that you could only think about becoming ONE with them? To me, that is what sex is: INTER-course, *to enter*. A self-directed need to join flesh and spirit with another person. Up to this point in my life, this has only happened with my own kind, but there are some Rakum who have such an attraction to mortals. But back to Tole.

We left Pitch on the ground and I instructed Bekan to stay with him, serve him when he awoke. With a self-deprecating shrug, Tole showed me to his sleeping quarters. The building appeared old and ill-kept, but in here, Tole's room was tidy, clean, and spacious. We were both slippery with sweat and dirt and I happily followed him to his bathroom.

"That thing Pitch said," he offered as he reached for my belt.

"Yeah," I returned and dropped a lazy eye to watch

70

his fingers.

During the fight, Pitch had accused Tole of being a horrible fuck. This hurt the guy for some reason which I read in his surface thoughts. Granted I only just met him, but most Rakum would not be fazed. We live to insult each other. But Tole had something to say, so I let him say it.

"I came into the world in 1800, separated from my pack by war and spent twenty years alone in the wilderness. I barely got enough blood and this stunted my development..." Tole spoke while unfastening my leather belt and then he pulled it free of the loops instead of moving to my fly. He paused to look up from his work and met my gaze. "Shit, your face..." he said in obvious awe. "I will never top this moment—looking at you, undressing you, before you find out how right Pitch truly was." Tole grinned on the last phrase, but I saw his pain.

"Go on," I said, meaning his story. He went for my fly.

"I was way past a century when I found my brothers again. They took me in, Master Blu finished my Ritual Training, but Pitch is right..." Tole slid my jeans off and did nothing else. I hadn't moved on removing his clothing and so he unhitched his own pants and dropped them. "Just let me enjoy this. I know I suck."

I gave him a smile and cupped his cheek with one hand. "Listen close. I'm the expert. Do you know this?" He nodded with round eyes. "Don't work. Relax. I will

71

not only fix this sadness, but also show you some cool tricks. You will blow Pitch away the next time he gets you in the sack." Tole did not react and I reached into his shower and turned on the water. "Say you believe me," I pressed.

"I believe you," he whispered.

Satisfied I walked him to the shower stall. It had been installed by the mortal designers with one occupant in mind, but we both stepped in and fit well enough. I didn't allow him to do anything, but bade he only receive. I promised I'd let him do more when the time was right, but he would never have such a perfect opportunity to be trained by the best. I used the shower experience to teach Tole the buildup; neither of us came and when I felt the time was right, I turned off the water and used the exact same amount of sultry attention that I had applied in the water to dry him off, head to toe.

I would not allow him to dry me—he needed to stop working. Did you see what I said there? He "needed." What does an ish-mikhan do but discern what a Rakum needs in order to be fixed?

So, I fixed Tole.

I walked that gorgeous 6'6" colossus to the bed and showed him my magic. When I finally allowed him to come, I walked him through a few tricks he could practice on me and surprise Pitch with later. The day was ten hours long and Tole and I played these games for half of those and then slept until sunset. When we awoke, we were holding hands and I sent him a mental 'kazak.' He squeezed my fingers and got out of bed. I have no doubt in my mind that if he had lived another twelve hours, he would have successfully worked all of these new things on his roommate.

But he died.

Read on because as I said, Rakum can live thousands of years. To die at 150? That's a damn shame.

Part II: Tole, He Died Well

Stupid. Stupid. Stupid.

When we arose, of course I had no idea he'd be gone by sunup. I'll walk you through it. As far as I know, none of my brethren have written about a Rakum's death, so it's pretty huge. I watched him dress, lying on my back, my head propped upon my arms. He moved like a tiger, strong and lithe, his long muscles leaner than mine, less bulky, more built for running. He liked that I watched him and when he caught my eye, he blushed like a mortal. That's damn sexy. As I mentioned, our brethren are hard and dark and grim; that's the way we're made. The ish-mikhan are more human, which makes us so very fuckable, but the rest of the brethren? Assholes. So that blush—fuck. Telling the story now, I wonder if I wouldn't have maintained some sort of attachment to Tole. My most compatible brother is Jersey, as some of you know, and I'm compatible with about a thousand to varying degrees. If Jersey is a 10/10, and Pitch is an excellent fuck at 7, I'd assign Tole a 9. Surprising, eh?

Tole was fully dressed when I heard Pitch coming. Our brother was down the hall and heading close so I concentrated on his heart sounds to determine his mood. Before he reached the open door, I sent him a silent 'kazak.' He ignored me and appeared, hands to his hips, his amazing eyes with those long eyelashes drawn small.

"Are you sorry you chose this puuta[12] over me?"

I was about to answer and Bekan stepped into view, behind Pitch and to the side. He sent me a kazak and I read in his eyes that Pitch had fucked him during their sleep period.

"I hope you paid attention," I sent to Bekan's mind and he shrugged, indicating he did his best for a guy with no sex drive. I had to giggle, but not amused, Pitch's eye remained hard.

"Come on," Pitch barked, overhearing my thoughts. "You'll come with us on our rounds."

I tossed back the sheet and prepared to dress. Pitch collected my clothing from the floor to hand it over. He looked at me when he was close and I winked again.

"From now on, you're in my bed. Do you understand?" he asked as stern as any Elder.

"Your will is my will," I said making sure he heard every syllable in my silkiest voice.

---

[12] Worthless person, (Rakum Hungarian)

Born in 1800, Pitch was younger, but he outranked me in military career, plus…I favored him. Just looking at him sent signals to my lower half. He saw this in my mind and his mouth formed the tiniest grin.

"But Tole might have you beat after our session; you better treat me right," I teased and he rolled his eyes.

I got dressed and Pitch sent Bekan and Tole to prepare the vehicle. Then, he escorted me to the underground garage. Along the way, he chided, "None of your prima donna shit. I don't have a limo."

"So long as I'm comfortable," I said and meant it. I should have allowed him to finish preparing me for his idea of transport. Two steps into the dank space and I spied an aged box truck. I stopped my forward motion. "*Hell* no."

"T, Beek, you're in back," Pitch called as he headed for the driver's seat.

I remained in place. Here's where I mention my disdain for undue discomfort. Since being identified in my specialty, little Darcy was moved "inside." *Inside* the proctor's bed, *inside* the master's favor; I was coddled. Hell—I was *fucking cuddled* from age nine on. Like any Rakum, I love violence and pain—but be uncomfortable? I pondered all of this, my right eye twitching, and Pitch aborted his movement, changed direction, and swiveled to the passenger side door. He opened it wide with a dramatic swish and bowed low.

"Oh, *polsz'v* extraordinaire, your chariot awaits

your delicious ass," he cooed from his downward posture.

That brought a grin and I consented. Tole and Bekan were in and secured the double door access from inside. Pitch buttered my bread by blowing me a kiss as he closed my door. He was teasing, but he knew I was royalty among the Rakum. Plus, ish-mikhan with no Elders around chose who they did and didn't fuck. This gave me power that I wielded with great joy.

We got underway and once Pitch had us on the main drag, my hunger rumbled. The clock struck eight and around us, the town had come alive with mortals filling restaurant plans. I decided that I wanted steak and two high-end eateries loomed ahead.

"Stop up there; get me a ribeye."

Pitch drove past with a tsk. "How much money did you bring?" He shot me a glance and looked back to the road. "We're not bankers and we stay broke."

My mouth went to the side; another apparent punishment for Darcy Vandiver. My Elder wanted me to miss him and the comforts his presence brought.

Well-played, Master Bel.

Still, it sucked. My stomach twisted as I imagined going without.

"Dammit, Pitch, I want a fucking steak," I said in a hiss. "Rob a bank, knock over a convenience store, do something and quick. I want a fucking ribeye or I'm moving on to the next waystation."

Pitch returned a slew of expletives, mostly pertaining to what a pussy his new ish-mikhan friend had become. I only smiled because my superior telepathy told me he was working something up that would get us paid. Then he was speaking to Tole, not intentionally barring me from hearing, but Tole's thread was too weak for me to latch on. I waited with one hand to my middle. Finally, Pitch shot me a new glare.

"Tole has a Cow who works for a local bookie. He'll help us take what's on hand."

"Excellent," I said with a sincere nod.

Pitch found a place to reverse and we headed in the opposite direction to the west end of town. Almost to the docks, he pulled into a dark alley. When he hopped down from the truck, I did too, and we met Tole and Bekan exiting the box.

"Over here," Tole said low and led the way deeper into the alley, the late fall wind whipping through the narrow space. Pitch, me, and Bekan bringing up the rear, we walked until we met a smallish man who approached Tole with his hands clasped behind his back and his eye filled with love for his master.

I must remark what a queer-looking guy this Cow was. Besides being only five-and-a-half feet tall, he had shaved his head and eyebrows and his beady eyes were much too close together. I whispered in our language that he looked like a cartoon, which garnered an agreeing giggle from Bekan. Tole peeked my way, bared his teeth to tap the surface and then pointed to the Cow's face.

"Worth his weight in gold," he whispered, again, in Rakum Hungarian.

I returned my attention to the Cow as he described his boss and the security details. He noted my scrutiny and looked at me. He melted a little at the eye contact, then—still talking to the others—he flashed a little grin.

"Hah," I huffed. The man had no center teeth, top or bottom.

"Houghton Street, Master, number 44," he was busy telling Tole. "Mr. F. runs B-ball there and tonight he'll haul in ten, fifteen grand, easy."

I watched the Cow's mouth, each word lisped due to his toothless state. I imagined him sucking off his master with that warm mouth. *Worth his weight in gold, indeed...*

He was still explaining. "All you gotta do is walk into the building like you own it." Toothless flashed me a flirtatious look. "Once in the lobby, there are two armed men watching a center door. Past there is a long hall with one guard watching the only door. Past him you'll find the counting room. The money already bundled is in the safe beneath the portrait of Kennedy. This room will have the accountant—he's old and harmless—and a woman, Kimmy, who helps him. She's Mr. F's wife."

In another minute, Tole had all the intel he required and Toothless offered him his blood. No Rakum says no to that, so the three of us waited for Tole in the truck and then we got underway. It took us fifteen minutes to reach the bookie's hideaway and once there, we parked on the side of the building out of sight and waited, giving Toothless an additional ten minutes to reach his post on the other side of town so he'd have an alibi for our heist.

Then it was time to go in. The building was not guarded from the sidewalk and we walked in as Toothless suggested. It had been an apartment complex with two units on each floor, one on each side of the front doors. The center door that the two guards watched was an addition, blocking what used to be an open hallway.

"Semi-automatic, extended mag, 9mm, with silencers," Pitch sent and I had noticed the same. He informed Tole telepathically and I did the same for Bekan behind me, even though he had no military training.

This is a good time to remind you what these two mortal guards were seeing. Tole and I being tall and broad-chested, would have looked to them like pro-ballers, maybe running backs, where Pitch was built more like the quarterback with lean muscle for quick movement plus endurance. And when they spied little Bekan, they'd think he was a kid, barely fifteen. Also, none of us were armed and the cut of our clothing revealed as much. The guards weren't as big or as tall as me or Tole, but they were hard, their eyes revealing they'd pulled their trigger plenty of times and were accustomed to the smell of blood and gunpowder.

"Hey, is this the bakery?" Pitch asked, diverting the men's attention as it would take only a split-second for two Rakum soldiers to assess the scene. The guards turned their weapons toward us, their fingers to the side of their triggers, revealing more than they could ever comprehend—these two were professional and they feared making a mistake. This meant they feared their boss and would think through issues that came upon them. Pitch and I would use this to our advantage, already gauging the men's skills and determining what level of effort would be required to end these men of violence. A brother can move in a blur, much faster than any mortal, but we must coordinate to ameliorate the risk of Rakum injury. I was looking at two men, two guns, and an unknown number of projectiles. Our plan was decided and shared with our two non-military brethren—Pitch and I would surge at the exact same time, and since we can speak telepathically, we worked that out.

It was time to begin. Tole put a hand to Bekan's shoulder which the guards interpreted as a possible provocation. Our window shrank to half as the men's fingers moved to cover their triggers, preparing to fire. The word "prepare" was their downfall being all the hesitation we needed to win the battle. Pitch and I surged into them faster than they could react, breaking their necks with our palms, their weapons dropping harmlessly to the ground. Pitch and I each lifted a dead man to use as a shield and kicked open the hall door. The guard inside stood just as Toothless described but he hadn't heard our assault. He scrambled for his firearm and got two shots off before we met him, shoving the bodies of his pals into his front, pressing him against the door behind him. His gun had a silencer, but the scuffle alerted a man inside for I heard him calling if the guard was okay. Pitch dropped his dead man to twist the gunman's head on its stem. He went down and now we needed to quiet the accountant

Pitch kicked open the door and we took cover assessing the room. I leapt left and concealed behind a large filing bank, Pitch and Bekan dove right, finding furniture to hide behind and Tole hugged the wall behind me near the door. The accountant did not have time to scream. He filled his lungs and Pitch zoomed into his space and broke his neck.

I grinned at my brother. So easy! Pitch pointed to the safe and Bekan went to work, dropping to the floor to listen and twirl the knob. An excellent locksmith, we knew he'd have it open in less than a minute. Tole stepped close to me and we bumped foreheads smiling like idiots.

But I forgot about the woman.

I smelled her then, and Tole did, too. We turned our face to the closed door, picking up not only a feminine aroma but the signature of bodily fluids. The boss's wife, presumably, was in the closet having surreptitious sex.

Click click click click click thunk. The safe was open and all three of us looked over Bekan's shoulder at a pile of money five times larger than Toothless predicted.

With silent cheers we met eyes, but my subconscious listened to the woman and her supposed lover. I heard heartbeats. Something was off. They were not racing. Breathing, but not as someone inflamed with lust. I met Pitch's eye and he also turned his face for the closet.

"They're being so quiet," he sent to my mind and I pondered it.

Why? She wouldn't fear that accountant. And probably not those guards either.

Pitch's eyes widened, his mind on the same track. *"Is her husband on the premises?"*

If so, the woman was as brazen as she was stupid. And then—in that second—no one felt more stupid than your friend Darcy as two things happened at once. A man shouted, "WHAT THE FUCK!" at the same time as seventeen live rounds penetrated the counting-room door in rapid, machine-gun-fire succession.

The four of us dove for cover in different directions, each to a wall, flattening against it and watching the hole-ridden door. It was kicked open and Bekan only inches away, went into action, all one hundred and twenty pounds of him. My valet yanked the firearm from the shooter and swung it like a bat, fracturing his skull with an echoing CRUNCH!

The boss and his last gunman dropped low to take cover behind tables and cabinets framing the room entrance. I could reach the boss and he hadn't seen me, so I flew into his space, grabbing him into a headlock from behind. I did not wait to see how long until he suffocated. I squeezed my elbow closed and his neck bones shattered with an audible crackle. In my peripheral vision and at the very same moment I snuffed out the boss, the final thug trained his gun barrel to Bekan's temple. On my best day, I couldn't outpace a bullet so I shouted for him to duck. Tole had seen it, too. With amazing speed, my newest lover lobbed the closest weapon he could grab—a metal stapler—and it flew like a missile to the man's head. When it made contact, the gunman fell, spasming in the throes of death without having pulled the trigger.

Bekan spun around, noticed what happened and jumped to Tole's side as he came to his feet. Tole turned to check Pitch and I noted an enlarging red circle marking his shirt. Bekan saw the same thing and lifted the hem to reveal a nasty exit wound. I jumped close to accelerate his healing with my touch, but I had forgotten about the woman.

And in these moments of what we considered entertainment, all four of us neglected to wonder why we didn't smell a male lover. The closet door burst open to reveal two women, half-dressed and disheveled, standing front to front. One of them was turning to face us. As we looked toward the movement, the woman lifted a rifle and fired the weapon point-blank, striking Tole in the forehead.

Tole. Tole. Tole...

There is a thread that ties the Rakum together. When one of us dies, it snaps. I found out this night that the pain of this is palpable. Pitch, Bekan and myself flinched, Bekan with a yelp, and with no thought other than KILL THOSE BITCHES, I moved in. Before they could take another breath, with my left and right hands to either woman's cheek, I slammed their heads together, smashing their faces into one. Deceased, the females slithered to the floor. I turned, my chest heaving with rage.

Pitch took charge and directed our exit strategy. "Beek, the money. Darss, bring Tole."

I lifted my brother from the tile and hefted him over my shoulder as my valet bagged more than fifty thousand dollars. We shuttled out the way Toothless had suggested and in minutes, we were in the dark alley between buildings. Remaining in the shadows, we jogged to the van and piled in, not witnessed by a soul. Since I was carrying Tole, I hopped into the box and Bekan and Pitch moved to the cab.

All the way to the waystation, I held my brother's head in my lap. At this point in history, I was 255 years old and had never witnessed a brother's death. Rakum don't care for each other like mortals, so his death was an inconvenience. Up front, I clearly saw Pitch's thoughts were on how to replace his assistant. Bekan was thinking, *We didn't get that steak. I wonder if we'll go out later...* But me? I have already admitted that ish-mikhan feel things more deeply than the other grunts. I was looking into Tole's face, *missing* him, longing to hear him laugh, and desiring very much to look into his gorgeous eyes as I worked him over.

But he was gone.

At the waystation, Pitch and I moved Tole's body to the basement where Pitch and Bekan dismembered him. Then, as per ancient protocol (to prevent mortals from finding his body), his separate parts were scattered in the building's outdoor courtyard. It was fenced and locked so when the sun came up, our brother's flesh would melt into the grass.

I'll close the telling; it makes me sad to recall it. I remained with Pitch a month before Elder Bel called me home. Bekan was assigned to remain with Pitch and I did not see him again except at Assembly. I would reconnect with Pitch many times, even to this day. I'll call him now. He'll lift my spirits.

But still. Poor Tole.

7

Sex in The Pelican

IT IS TIME TO SHARE ABOUT MY NEXT CANAAN
ENCOUNTER. I saw my favorite Elder only
intermittently because the Fathers determined we needed
to be kept apart. This was for my own good. Canaan
didn't think about me when out of sight, but when I bed
down each dawn, his face or chest or other parts would
flash across my mind. I had thousands of brothers to
sleep with (and I enjoyed them all), but as it is with
mortals—the chemistry between us kept me at a steady
state of readiness to see him again.

All that doesn't mean I pined in the way mortals
do. Still, if I caught his scent on a brother, I'd ask for an
update. If I heard his name spoken, I'd lean in and

insinuate myself into the conversation. I am happy my face and status allowed me generous favor because I could never get enough information on Elder Canaan.

In 1979, I took an assignment to accompany Rand, Bel's top lieutenant, to New York City. I was there for Rand's pleasure, but he preferred women which helped in his mission to inspect the Elder's brothels in the Big Apple.

The third evening in town, I tailed him to a few establishments and stood by as he did his job. Each brothel housed two Cows minimum, and this night, both Cows were women which made the blood meal especially wonderful. Rand and I tapped the Cows and faced the exit, both of us wondering where to go next.

"Work is done, time to play, Hotstuff," he said. He then put his finger to his eye. I'd known him two years and recognized his quirks—he'd been contacted by our master. I waited with a raised brow and he gave me a secret grin. "Bel loves picking on you, doesn't he?"

"That he does," I replied grinning. If Bel had cooked up some abuse, I was ready to dive in—his pleasure my priority. Elder Canaan's name flashed across Rand's mind in the present tense and my dick jumped. "He's in town?"

Rand smiled again. "At The Pelican. Let's go." And my lieutenant headed away, me jogging to keep up. Oh shit, I could barely control my joy at the idea of a reunion.

The Pelican was a rowdy bar Elder Jack Dawn owned and was popular among the brethren. We allowed mortals inside, but Dawn allowed fighting and violence, the police were bought and never came to the aid of whiners. As a result, only the toughest men and lowest dregs of humanity came in. Just enough of their kind to keep us entertained as we behaved like the brutes we are.

On the drive to Battery Park where the establishment sat nestled between two Korean restaurants, Rand attempted to provoke me with teases involving my past with Canaan. He would never disrespect a master, but he duly enjoyed dragging my name through the worst insults to see if he could stoke my ire. If I had wanted to fight, I would have allowed his words to affect me, but all I could think of was Canaan pulling me close for a kiss.

Hah—go ahead and laugh. You caught me—Elders don't do that with any sort of affection. But as we've established, I'm a romantic. In my mind, Canaan puts his hands to either side of my neck, tells me how much he missed me, and tenderly touches our lips. We melt together over a few seconds and…

Rand punched my near arm as hard as he could and the recoil knocked me into my side of the car.

"FUCK!" I barked and swiveled to slam a balled fist into his shoulder the same measure. But we had arrived and Rand put the car in park. He didn't make a move to get out, but instead grunted for me to look his way.

"Lean over," he commanded when our eyes met. With my brow raised, I complied. "Closer you shit," he added roughly grabbing my neck. With a quick yank, his face sunk into my neck and he took a long swipe with his tongue, from the collar of my shirt to my ear lobe and pushed me away with a wicked grin. "Now, get out, and come around to my side of the truck."

With a soft chuckle, I did as instructed. Not only is Rand my superior in military rank, but also being ten years older, my master by age. Plus, I was curious at what he was up to. I wasn't too surprised at his comical leanings; I found Rand humorous all the time. He was the type of Rakum that used humor to his advancement, and he was very good at it. With part of my brain walking into the bar to see Canaan, I came around to Rand's side and opened the door.

"Good," Rand said and swiveled to see me. He parted his knees to invite me to step closer, him still sitting in the truck. He reached for my jacket and pulled me all the way in. "Open your pants." Rand didn't break into a laugh, but I sensed he was close. I wondered where he was going; surely not to perform anything sexual. He had something up his sleeve. I unbuttoned my jeans. "Be still."

I watched my lieutenant lick his hand from the heel of his palm to his fingertips and shove it down the front of my pants. With practiced ease, he manipulated my every inch, not removing his fingers until I had stiffened, grinning with surprise.

"Let's see how your master likes that," he said with a chuckle.

I fastened my pants shaking my head. "He'll never be anywhere near my cock," I said backing so he'd exit the driver's seat. The fact of the matter is, Elder's *receive* pleasure, they do not give it. Canaan would never touch a grunt's dick. No Elder would. The end.[13]

"But he'll kiss your neck," Rand said.

I gave a shrug. He would and I couldn't wait to feel his lips on my throat. My muse tugged me then; the Elder was tired of waiting and I needed to get inside. I released a tiny sigh as Rand took his time adjusting his clothing and kicking dust from his boots. "If you're finished licking me, our master's await."

Rand agreed with a chortle and we were stopped by a shout from the entrance.

"Assholes! Come in or get the fuck out of the parking lot!—" The man stopped short, recognizing us as Rakum. Rand called him over in our language, ending with, "...and look what we have here."

I turned my face as the brother approached. He was 6'3", bronze-skinned and hirsute, his stern features giving him the appearance of a proud Indian warrior. He

---

[13] So I do not seem disingenuous, at this time in my life, I believed this to be true. Jersey later claimed otherwise (*Blood, Sex, & Violence, A Vampire's Rebuttal, p.120*). ~ Darcy

met my eye and cursed.

"You're fucking kidding me! Darcy Vandiver? I got that right, right?" he asked knowing the answer. I hadn't met him before, but his intonation meant he knew my reputation. He put one hand to his chest. "I'm Dahkus, Elder Blu's pack," he said. "And you're goddamn gorgeous. And so big! Shit!"

His eyes flit to Rand who nodded. I was not fazed by his adulation, my middle pulling me to the bar. Dahkus stepped aside, his respect evident. Rand had a notion to add to his earlier tease and commanded me to stand still. In Rakum Hungarian, he told Dahkus to kiss my neck. The handsome brother moved in and I leaned down to make it easier. He wanted more, so much more, and the silly edict to kiss a fix-it man who was obviously already on a mission did not force back his libido. After a moment, he opened his mouth against the skin, laving with gusto.

At that moment, all three of us heard a telepathic command from an Elder inside (not Canaan) and we broke contact. Rand slapped my behind and passed me for the entrance leaving me and the bouncer to walk together.

"Darcy, are you staying at the waystation on Bleeker?" he asked without slowing our pace. I said we were, but only for two more nights. "Judas Priest, let me come visit you. I'll bring gifts. Fuck!" he hiss-whispered.

I enjoyed that last part—they never brought me

presents. "I like chocolate," I said without joking and with the tiniest nod, he opened the door and I left him at the stoop to guard the entry.

This was it. I was entering alone—just as I had in my fantasy. The Pelican was boisterous tonight, like most nights, the patronage varied from my brethren, to Cows, to a few females there on business. The soldier in me counted heartbeats, revealing twenty-five mortals and twenty-two Rakum—three of those, Elders. Again, a tingle rushed to my dick and my eyes sought the bar. I peered past the bodies; across the busy establishment, three Elders sat upon stools, their backs to me and their faces in the mirror. Elder Greco and Elder Thorn flanked Canaan and reading their eyes in the reflection, they knew I was for their brother Canaan. I had been with them both over the years. Then, like in my fantasy, they laughed and jabbed Canaan's arm.

"Who called for a sex doll?" Thorn asked in our language. I started for the bar and halfway there, Elder Canaan turned in his stool and met my eye.

Fuck. There it was.

His eyes spoke volumes and the tales they told were my entire world. I waited for his script—he would say it. I only had to wait. He slid to the floor and stood.

"Come close, pup," he said, and I exhaled, unlocking my feet. I came close the way he liked, slow and catlike, oozing sex and the promise of pleasure. Experience told me he loved this part and I did not

92

disappoint. His grin went to the side and behind him, the other two masters laughed. Then, my fantasy ended abruptly when Canaan stopped four strides out and put up his palm. His eyes narrowed and trained then over my shoulder. "Is that motherfucking Rand on you? And…" Canaan sniffed the air. "And the fucking bouncer?"

I didn't answer his rhetorical queries. Canaan passed me as if I did not exist, on a new mission to smash the brothers who dared mock him. My place was to wait for his timing, so I continued to the bar where Elders Thorn and Greco welcomed me to sit between them.

"Darcy, you look well," Thorn said and ruffled the hair at the crown of my head.

"What the fuck are you saying?" Elder Greco chimed in. "He looks *perfect.*"

"Thank you, Masters," I said and then read the plan the Elders concocted in real-time.

Somewhere behind us, Canaan had laid hands on Dahkus. I heard a crash of furniture, a mortal yelped with surprise and quieted, and then the Elder barking for Rand to join him in the fighting chamber.

"Come, little brother." Elder Thorn's cool fingers encircled my wrist. "Will you entertain your masters while Canaan plays with your brethren?"

"Your will is my will," I replied and moved away from the bar, following the master's lead. Greco was directly behind and once we passed the mortals and headed down the long hallway, his hand conformed to my backside. The ish-mikhan spirit inside divined my masters' needs and prepared an order of go, while at the same time, my heart pouted, imagining Canaan close and all the ways I might make him smile.

"Shit, that's the sweetest thing I've ever *not* heard a brother say," Thorn mused, now reaching a door so low that I ducked to enter. "I should smash you for that weak shit."

Greco laughed. "Let him pine. It's sexy as fuck. And hurry, you walk like an old Cow."

Thorn headed down a short flight of stairs. Being in Battery Park, a manufactured island, the hand-dug cellar was not more than six feet high and I lowered to enter the musty space with my masters. The floor was dirt and the walls covered with plywood and supported by steel joists.

"Okay, my beautiful ishy," Greco said. "How will you fix me?"

He didn't need to ask, but it pleased him to hear his own voice, the tight space providing an entertaining echo. Thinking of voices reminded me my masters hadn't heard me speak more than a greeting tonight. When I served them in the past, Thorn was much more aroused by my hands on his body, but Greco fell apart at my voice. My muse begged me to please them both, so I decided I would. It was a risk—the one who didn't care so much about my voice could strike out and cancel my service by knocking me unconscious. I moved ahead with my plan and turned to meet Greco's eye in the light thrown by the single muslin torch.

"Master," I said grabbing Greco's huge brown eyes, "whatever I have is yours." My voice reverberated in the small space and my master was hard before I finished my first sentence. "It is because of you that I live. Because of you, I wake up every sunset and dream of your face..."

The man was done—enraptured by my tongue. Thorn listened, too, and his hand slid to the back of my throat.

"Me, first," he whispered sounding parched.

But I wasn't done.

"Master, let me show you..." I turned my eyes to Thorn. "Let me show you how much I adore and worship you."

And no one spoke again. Both masters found themselves speechless and at my mercy as I showed them both why my reputation preceded me across our race. In fifteen short minutes, both were panting with surprise and elation at what I had accomplished with their flesh.

"Judas Priest! I forgot!"

That was Thorn speaking to Greco, leaning against the wall with his eyes half-closed. I leaned against the stair rail awaiting the next command and listening for Canaan. Then all three of us heard him asking where I had gone.

"You didn't forget, brother," Greco said to Thorn, not caring that I overheard. "You don't get enough quality head."

"If the Fathers loaned this one to me a month…" Thorn said smiling and he turned his face to the low ceiling.

"Elder Bel doesn't loan him out," Greco said and closer to the cellar door, Canaan cursed them for taking me away while he fought.

Thorn slapped his palm to his eyes and laughed. "Bel is the stingiest motherfucker I know." Then he turned his gaze my way. "What do you say we turn this beautiful ishy over to Canaan?"

Thorn turned his pointer finger in an upside-down circle, indicating I should go upstairs. I did and the Elders followed close behind.

"Go see the Elder, little brother," Thorn said.

I reached for the doorknob to the main floor and the door pulled outward. Elder Canaan stood in the space, larger than life, standing above me as I was still on the stairs. And his eyes. *Shit.* That look—I could live forever in his gaze. He was a master, his power and might more than I could comprehend, but his eyes spoke a language my muse interpreted with ease.

I want you. I need you.

And my favorite of all,

I missed you.

It doesn't matter if the Elder realized this. I did.

And I was the one with the oversized human tendencies. I would see altruism and love before any of my brethren, and my favorite master had it bad.

"You're just not all that, Vanny," he said in a whisper. But I think he was speaking for the other Elders. His gaze said I was all that, and so much more.

"Master, let me serve you," I said at the same volume.

"Yes, I think that would be best." He raised his eyes to those of the Elders coming up behind me and added, "You know where to go. Wash and wait for me."

Without delay, I passed him and he followed with his eyes. That was worth everything in the world, that he watched me go, and when I could no longer see him in my peripheral vision, I felt his eyes on my back. I was in heaven.

Because this is my memoir and I do what I want, I'm going to share with you another little fact. Now that I'm human, I can see much that I couldn't see before. Now that I'm human, I can tell you with 100% certainty that at that time *Canaan loved me.* Rakum did not love, we had no selflessness (which is what human love is), but now that I'm mortal, I see that's what it was. He would never have been able to act on it because of his Rakum nature, but the human seed inside of him loved me.

So, to belabor the point no longer, I showered to erase the aroma of my brethren. When I was clean and emil jersey

had towel dried my hair, I left the bathroom, listening for Canaan's heart sounds. Opposite the pub were private rooms and I followed his sounds to the proper door and pushed it open. The space was spotless, a bedroom, but with only a bed and one chair, as if designed specifically for sex. Its immaculate condition belied that this room was reserved for Elders and the oversized bed emanated a gentle aroma of freshly laundered sheets.

Where was Canaan? He was there, but I couldn't see him. Not yet. The door closed on its own and my master materialized in the dark corner. Elders can't "disappear" like the Fathers, but they are able to dampen their presence—a mental, telepathic blindness they project onto others which prevents being seen. I turned to meet his eye and my smile was enormous. This I know because Elder Canaan reflected it on his own handsome face.

"Vanny…"

He spoke the word with such exasperation, such desperation, that I was immediately hard as a rock.

"Vanny," he said again, his voice low and rumbling with testosterone, "for the love of the Fathers, come close…"

And I did.

Elder Canaan and Darcy Vandiver reconnected in The Pelican. *Judas Priest*, did we reconnect…

98

The Messenger

THIS CHAPTER MAY GO OVER THE HEADS of some readers, but just as many of you experience the same deep soul searching as I do.

This one's for you.

The Messenger showed up at Last Assembly. I couldn't have known we would end up calling it that, but at the end of that meeting, my entire race scattered and was never the same again. I will share the tale of The Messenger without divulging major plot points of the Rabbit Saga. Let's dive in.

The Rakum gathered for Assembly at the Fathers' whim, usually once every decade. In late 2011, we had several months before the next scheduled gathering, so when this impromptu session was called, I had been in Los Angeles, California, on assignment and on loan to a lieutenant of Elder Brandon's named Sarna.

Sarna was big, not as tall as I am, but broad-chested, his middle thick with muscle, with enormous hands that he knew how to use, be it for pain or for pleasure. And this brother wore a full beard that I enjoyed to the utmost. When we made love, I would thrust the fingers of both hands in deep, weaving into the coarse curls, to jerk him close for kisses that lasted forever. Oh, shit, I need to stop.

Onto the story.

Sarna had been with Brandon since First Ritual, which wasn't too unusual; soldiers often stayed with the same Elder for life. In this season, Sarna found himself in Brandon's favor, so when asked who he would like to accompany him on his mission, he remembered his favorite fuck, *yours truly*. Lucky for him, my master had a new mate[14] and sent me along, knowing I'd return when the time was up. Because of this, Sarna and I reconnected in L.A. and made the best of our free time.

One evening after completing his duties, he and I turned in early to warm the sheets a few hours before sunup. There was no shortage of Cows in our adopted area, so we had fed well on blood and then rich foods, our bellies full and comfortably distended. To get Sarna to hurry, I undressed before he had even reached our quarters. By the time he crossed the threshold, I had slid

---

[14] Rakum don't "marry" but are permitted to take a mate. We bore easily so it's usually a *very* short tenure. ~ Darcy

beneath the covers and propped my head on my hands.

"No way, not this time," he warned, half-joking because the last time we were naked, I went an entire round by myself. "Don't move a muscle, asshole," he said and whipped off his jacket and then his button-down shirt.

Because of his barking command, with a teasing lip smack, I snaked one hand down my front beneath the sheet.

"No, Darcy! Fuck it! Stop right now!" he shouted, working down his jeans, a growing fury in his rumbling, throaty voice.

I grinned wider and did not stop prepping my machine.

He stumbled out of his boots on his way to the bed. "Hands up, motherfucker! Get your goddamn hands where I can see them!"

I laughed at his TV-Cop script, but he was dead serious. He flew into me, physically yanking out my missing wrist and pinning both arms to the headboard. He straddled my torso, his buttocks resting across my bellybutton and I laughed as he tried to kiss my mouth, leaning low. I moved out of reach, laughing, tossing my head side to side, dodging his efforts. No matter how fiercely he held my wrists to the oak, there was no controlling my other movements.

"Goddammit, Darcy! Be still! I'm gonna toss if you don't stop fucking around and BE STILL!"

I laughed harder thinking maybe he would vomit on me. *Sarna threw up on the ish-mikhan! Can you believe it?* I ran down a few more gossips and he bellowed one last command.

"NEW GAME! YOU'RE MADE OF STONE! DO IT NOW!"

Panting, sweat dripping from his brow to mine, he leaned over me, at the same time dropping the wrist hold. I did not move, holding his eye, my grin in place. I did not breathe, I did not blink. In less than fifteen seconds, his ire passed, his respirations returned to normal, his heart pounding because we were commencing the dance.

"Don't move. You're made of stone," he said again in a whisper, sliding back to my hips. *"This is my new favorite game..."* He had sent that thought silently and used both gigantic paws to stroke my chest and shoulders.

Then his cell rang with his master's assigned tone. No one ignores an Elder. Sarna slid free and jogged to where he'd left his phone. When he answered, I heard his master say in our language, *"Get to The Cave and call your people. Now."*

My phone also rang and I got the same message from Samson, Elder Bel's valet.

More curious than concerned, we forgot our playdate, dressed, and headed for the airport. I had been promoted to lieutenant some years before, so like Sarna, I also had men under me to alert. In the hired car, we phoned our subordinates. Our captains would call their top men, on down the line until every Rakum knew to beat a path to Nevada.

Why use phones? If you're reading my memoir before the rest of *The Rabbit Saga Collection Series*, you may not realize that although many of us (myself included) have extraordinary telepathic abilities, the grunts (anyone not an Elder or Father) were unable to dependably call each other long distance. It varied between each man, but I was able to contact favored brethren up to fifty miles away. Jersey could reach only about ten miles. In contrast, if we were in his pack an Elder could touch any of us at any time. He could also reach brothers outside of his pack, but at varying strengths. (Side note: Our Fathers were connected to all 100,000 24/7/365, living vicariously through their offspring, able to explode any of us with a thought. They never did, but we knew they had the power. Just so you know.)

On to the calling of my men. I set the chain reaction as we headed for LAX. Our people had light-tight private jets that could take a Rakum anywhere without reservations, so we headed for the proper terminal, brilliantly disguised as an exclusive foreign shipping company. By the time we reached the gate, seven other brothers had gathered from the surrounding counties and we piled into the waiting CRJ.

There were no Elders on the flight, and since Sarna

and I outranked the others, we sat in the cushy first-row captain's chairs while the remaining brethren filled the common seats.

"What have you heard?" Sarna asked the highest-ranking soldier who filled the seat directly behind him.

"There's trouble with a Rabbit," the man said and had no other information. I looked to my companion's face and he could add nothing else. Neither of us were aware of any such trouble and as the jet taxied down the runway, individually, we phoned our people for intel. I re-dialed Samson. He had already arrived which only proved how late Sarna and I were receiving the news.

"When you get here, proceed directly to our seating. No one has details, but it surrounds Elder Dawn and a Rabbit he marked. Hurry. Kazak."

Sarna found out even less than I had and we both faced front and fell into our thoughts. The other men did, too, and we had a short hop in silence.

Since 1950, "The Cave" was the Rakum headquarters, an intricately carved tunnel system beneath the Nevada desert (also known as Area 51) purchased from the U.S. government. We operated a facility down there full time, producing different products the mortals used in the aerospace industry.

Before tonight, we always enjoyed Assembly. An ish-mikhan was a superstar at these gatherings; think of it, a hundred thousand Rakum crammed into barracks and suites for however long our masters demanded. Do you see how desperately my brethren might need a fix-it man? This is why Jersey, Hester, Julio, and myself usually adored the mandatory gatherings.

But not this time.

No one was thinking about fucking, fighting, or taking a live buzz.[15] Upon disembarking in the underground hangar, Sarna and I made our way to the main hall. He split off to the right to sit with his pack and I headed to the east end, upper level, where I'd find Elder Bel's. I settled in with my brothers and faced the stage.

Without providing spoilers, just know that someone who was not a Rakum stood on the Fathers' bema and informed us that there was a Maker. He loved us and wanted us to spend eternity with Him.

Yeah.

Right.

We didn't care about any of that shit, and when we were permitted to leave our seats, I did.

Had this been a normal Assembly, I would have slept in an Elder's suite, but I sensed none of our masters near. What this meant, I didn't know, and truly, I did not want to know just yet. Something had happened to our race and I couldn't tell yet what it was. My spirit felt hollow, alone, and small. I couldn't speak to my pack

---

[15] A live buzz is blood taken off a mortal who does not die from the process. FYI: A dying buzz (blood taken from a mortal who will die while you drink) is forbidden because of the negative affect it has on the brother who commits the crime. A dead buzz is blood pulled from a corpse. Not recommended if you want to look pretty. Ahem.

members about it, and none of them confided in me.

Even with the unfamiliar trauma sensation wracking my soul, my cells informed me the sun would be up in an hour. I'd need to remain below ground and figure it out up top at dusk. I toddled to the dorm wing seeing nothing but my own concerns.

Upon arrival, our bunker was deserted. I barked a few curses, seeking the three of my pack members who had been with me in the Main Hall minutes before. Where the shit had they gone? When no one replied, I grumbled my way to the nearest bunk and fell atop the rough wool blanket. It was wholly shitty sleeping alone. Fuck! On the most stressful evening of my long life and my idiot brethren clung to each other elsewhere. For the first time in my life (and thankfully the *only* time), I was a regular guy. And I *hated* it.

The sleeping quarters were dimly lit by low-wattage yellow bulbs in the rock ceiling and I stared at them, pondering all that I had heard and seen and felt.

I felt what?...

When the person on the stage told us about the Maker, my ears listened. The promises and assertions this person made about who and what and how the world came into being rang true, *but why should I care?*

This is what disturbed me as I attempted to doze away the hours—what did all of that have to do with me?

❖ ❖ ❖

I awoke with a start and sat up. One glance confirmed that I was still alone, every bunk empty. I got to my feet to look at the open door. The hallway was empty and as quiet as the room in which I stood.

Quiet.

Quiet?

It was *too* quiet. I heard no heartbeats.

Where was everybody?

I traversed the long hall, the rough-hewn rock walls glistening with water, the floor made of smoothed bedrock and chest high light-strips delineating each hall. I reached the elevator at the end of Barracks 3 and still, I heard no hearts. I boarded the lift. This box opened to the foyer outside the hangar, a room the size of two football fields. Surely some of my brethren were there, working out a plan. But no. Not a soul in sight, and still, I heard nothing but the sounds of The Cave, dripping water and humming machinery.

"Kazak l'pirzah!" I belted in our language, calling a greeting that included a plea for a reply.

"Over here," a smooth voice replied in English and I circumvented a humongous load-bearing pillar to see who spoke. It appeared to be a man with white-blonde hair past his shoulders, white eyebrows, and pale blue eyes. He wore grey coveralls and *very* shiny brown leather dress shoes. None of our NCJ pilots dressed this way and we did not employ mechanics.

Also, he wasn't a Rakum, for I'd know a brother

on sight. One sniff revealed he wasn't a mortal; he had no discernible odor (blood or body scent) or heart sounds. I was confounded. Was I afraid? Fuck, no. Remember who you're dealing with—Darcy Vandiver, Rakum Lieutenant, Elder Bel's favorite companion (wherever he was at the moment, I didn't know).

I looked at this "person" and checked off what or who it might be. As I did, he stepped toward me, gliding across the rough cement floor. He stopped fifteen feet away with a nod, tucking his hands into his pockets. He appeared calm and unthreatening. Then I noticed the other thing that proved he wasn't human—he had zero reaction to me as ish-mikhan.

No, all humans do NOT have to fawn over my face or body; I understand we all have our preferences. But this visitor's eyes never left mine; when I looked away, his gaze waited for mine to return. He exuded an interest in communicating with my mind alone, and that's as well as I can explain it.

One of us needed to speak, so I proceeded.

"Where is everyone?" I asked as that seemed the most pressing question.

"You overslept. They're all gone, left hours ago and the sun is upon you once more. Can you not feel it?" He said all of this in English and I detected no accent. At his last question, he shrugged and was truly asking.

I thought about the sun. My Rakum spirit usually "saw" its proximity to the horizon and from there I could gauge the safe time. My inner self returned no information and I shook my head.

"What the fuck is it to you?" I asked, no interest in making friends with the freak I couldn't identify. I considered that he might be an illusion. I didn't dream as a rule (most Rakum don't), but what if the crap that just happened worked a number on my brain?

"I hung around to see if you'd like to live a bit longer." Another shrug. "If you do, follow me. The Cave is being dismantled and a million tons of bedrock is about to fill this hangar."

I inhaled. And I didn't ask if he was shitting me. Another thing I can hardly explain about this guy was that when words left his mouth, I knew a zillion percent that he spoke the truth. I did not need to understand why that was at the moment; I needed to evacuate the space.

"Go," I said, which was all I could muster, my mind spinning.

Pause your reading to recall how odd this is – not the stranger; who gives a fuck about him? – no, my mind "spinning". Rakum live lives of certainty. No weak emotions of fear and worry and consternation. And even though I had more "feelings" than a non-fix-it man, I was never weak. The shit in my heart during this escape was *weakness*. And I hated it *so much!*

But I wanted to live.

The stranger turned and headed to the rear double-doors. I tailed him and once through, he avoided the elevator bank and broke into a jog for the STAIRS door. I'd been down those stairs. They led to a boiler room about twenty-by-twenty. As we descended, I watched the back of his head in the low light, his weird silk-like hair reflecting as if metallic. My mouth said, "What do they call you?"

"Judah," he replied, his face away navigating the extended tight stairwell.

They call him Judah, I said inside and he yanked open the final door. Above us a rumbling began and the stone steps vibrated beneath my boots. Judah did not have to tell me to hurry; when he increased his pace, I did too, trailing him to a small door, three-feet-by-three-feet.

I'd been in there, too. Not every Rakum knew about it, but this was one of several sneak away places the year-round brethren hid when off-duty. These impromptu tunnels were hand dug and personalize by the initial brainiac who desired it. Over the years, we found them and used them for anything we wanted to do alone. I'd been in there to fuck, but what else would you expect?

Judah tugged open the door as the walls of the boiler room shook and dropped fine dust atop our heads. He scooted in, crawling on all fours and I followed, my size giving me a shorter gait navigating the close tunnel.

Twenty-five feet in and the rumble reached our location, the light seeping in from the small door evaporating. Now in the pitch, I slowed my crawl to avoid bumping the stranger. My memory told me we were reaching the end and I stopped and slowly stood, hunched over, but I knew the tiny tunnel ended in a five-foot-high space.

I could see nothing, the dark a heavy blanket over my senses. I lifted my cell phone from my pocket and awoke the screen. There was no service underground, but the battery was full. Judah stood across from me, also hunching his six-foot height. Behind him was a boulder that when pushed aside, would reveal a hollowed-out chute to the surface. He blocked it with his body and grinned when I locked my gaze with his.

"You made it," he said as a secret. *"The Cave is no more. This space will hold another moon cycle before it collapses. At sundown, crawl out and go from there."*

I shook my head in disbelief. He was giving me last-minute instructions. Was he leaving? If so, how?

"You want me to wait with you?" he asked, his face illuminated by my cell. "You can ask me questions. Some I will answer, some I won't." He lowered to a hunker, sitting on his heels, then collapsed to his rump to sit cross-legged.

I also lowered and mimicked his posture, facing him, my arms relaxed in my lap. I set the phone, screen up, between us and pondered a few questions. I chose what seemed most urgent. "How long until sundown?"

What an idiot-sounding phrase from my mouth;

never (I mean NEVER), even as a pre-rit,[16] did I not know what time it was. But it is what it is, so I watched for his answer.

"Noon in Nevada."

The way he said "in Nevada" had me curious so I went with it.

"Where are you from?"

"Umm," he said with an eye twitch. "Next."

Okay. He said he'd answer some and not others. I had time, I'd ask whatever came out.

"You don't live in Nevada?"

He shook his head.

"What are you? You're not a man, right? Or is there something wrong with me?" This only occurred to me as I spoke. I did a quick check: my body sounded right, my strength felt right, my night-vision lit up the room with the limited illumination from the phone screen. My gut hungered for blood and solid food...

"Next." Judah held my gaze. He looked happy. I think he enjoyed my confusion, but what could I do? We were trapped together for several hours and I did not want to wait alone if he could somehow "leave" a rock tomb without opening the hatch.

"Why did you rescue me?" I asked.

"I think you're worth it," he said without inflection. "You have a lot of influence on your brethren. They

---

[16] Short for "pre-ritual grunt." A brother who hasn't graduated First Ritual.

listen to you. When you get back on track, remember that I see great things in you. Huge things you can't even imagine."

Finally, some emotion reached his eyes as he spoke the last few words. His luminescent eyes brightened, and his mouth formed a grin, revealing white teeth that may have been pointed—of this I'm not sure.

I was growing cognizant something bigger than me had happened. Bigger than the Rakum or the person on the stage sharing the story of the Creator.

"Are you a messenger from the Maker?" I asked as the thought occurred to my mind. He offered a more-or-less gesture. "You are a messenger of the Maker who saw Darcy Vandiver about to be crushed and you see his future." I watched his face for a reaction, and he gave the exact same response. Encouraged, I added, "My future is important to the Maker."

"All of you are important. You, in particular, have a good connection with your spirit. The Maker is connected to your soul, inserted there by the human breeder that birthed you. When you reconnect with your brothers tonight, remain open to the Maker's voice. Will you do this?"

"Will I recognize His voice?"

"Without a doubt." Judah leaned against the moist wall. With an absent nod, I also leaned back and softened my gaze to think. The cell screen timed out and I left it dark.

I will reconnect with my brothers…

Judah said it, so it was so. I would not be crushed.

My brothers left me.

I had gone to sleep alone and in their state of emergency, no one noticed their favorite fix-it man oversleeping in his bunk. I wasn't mad at them, but sorry I'd not found a bunkmate.

Thinking of bunkmates, I thought of Sarna. We had just started the ignition sequence when we received the call to head for The Cave. Where had he gone? I wished then that we were together. I'm not ashamed to admit that if I had a brother with me in that tiny space, I'd put him across my lap and hold him close.

I could maybe hold Judah…

That made me grin. The guy seemed *alien*. He would probably *zap* me if I should touch him. Judah chuckled in the pitch and I cocked my chin his way.

"Can you see my thoughts?" I asked, my voice soft.

"Yes," he answered, his voice echoing more than before in the lightlessness.

"The Maker can see them, too?"

"That's the beauty of making something. You made all of it, even its thoughts."

I considered his statement with a nod. "Are you the only messenger of the Maker?"

"No."

"Can all the messengers see my thoughts?"

"No."

Deductive reasoning had kicked in and I narrowed my eyes in the dark. "Are you the Maker?" I asked in a careful whisper. No answer. I waited, I listened. When he said nothing after sixty seconds, I bumped my phone screen. I was alone. I narrowed my eyes, letting this sink in and resisting what must be the truth of it. Then my phone chimed in my hand. There was no cell service, yet I received a message from non-indexed caller. I opened the app, my finger hovering over the words, "Unknown Sender". With a careful swallow, I touched it and a message opened. It read: *"I love you. I see your potential. Keep your ears open. ~ I am now Known."*

There you have it. The Maker's Messenger rescued Darcy Fucking Vandiver from the demolition of our Headquarters. I went to the surface when the sun was down and I hot-footed it to the road five miles across the desert. I hitched a ride from an elderly couple heading to Las Vegas and they dropped me off at one of our Elder's hotels. From there, I went looking for my brothers, *anyone would do,* and I didn't find them for a long time. When I finally ran across a brother, he moved into my hotel room and we hunkered low a very long time working to figure out what happened.

You can follow these events in *The Rabbit Saga,* but *Judas Priest!,* it was tough on us. Let's continue the memoir with what happened a few years afterward. It gets worse. Much worse. Sigh.

9

The Sexpert Goes Human

WHERE WERE YOU WHEN THE TWIN TOWERS
FELL? When Michael Jackson died? When all of the
Rakum turned human at the same time? My answers:
2001, playing poker with Pitch in New York; 2009,
Rough-housing with my master in Nevada; and lastly,
2018, in bed with an Elder-Candidate in Atlanta,
Georgia.

For his memoir, Jersey wrote about the night he
went human. He had his pants down and was seconds
away from coitus when it happened. How proper for an
ish-mikhan to go down while screwing! As you shall see,
your ish-mikhan friend Darcy Vandiver, also, will not
disappoint.

At Last Assembly (the event in the previous chapter), we lost our Rakum unity because of the events of the *Rabbit Saga* (I won't give you any major spoilers). But we were still fully Rakum, still vampires, still powerful, and I remained as sexy as I had always been. We had lost contact with our Fathers and Elders, so each grunt was on his own. We clumped together as best we could, and most of my brothers were miserable.

I was *not.*

No matter how sad the world had become, I always had my cock, and it made me (and anyone around me) joyful. Thus, in 2018 were separated but still Rakum, and the Elders I loved so well were dead or missing. Happily, I ran into Avel.

The ish-mikhan weakness has always been the Elders. Our very DNA craved them. Shit, you would read in Jersey's memoir how I discovered electricity bounced between my skin and Elder Canaan's. Literally! *Shit!*

After 2012 (also called "Last Assembly," for those who read the entire Saga), we scattered and I couldn't find the Elders. I had plenty of lovers, but my ish-mikhan spirit nightly sought my master's mental threads. Six years go by and my poor muse cried every sundown, reaching into the abyss left behind by our masters. Then, on November 1, 2018, while driving through downtown Atlanta, trolling for hookers or a quick lay, my muse switched on like a halogen beam.

"FUCK!" I barked, alone in the truck, and laughing

at myself when every part of my body went online seeking the cause of my sudden wood. It had been so many years and I did not want to be wrong about what my flesh spelled out. This expression of every follicle springing tall meant an Elder was near. I hated to think of the disappointment if I misread myself.

Then I saw him.

Fuck-fuck-fuck.

An Elder, or as close as I'd seen in years, strolled out of a bar, his arm around a woman. I didn't see her details, the Candidate's glory eclipsing all else in those first moments. I jumped the curb, threw the truck into park and leapt out. I even left the keys and the door ajar – who cares if it was stolen? Surely not me. I jogged up and milliseconds before I reached my goal, he spun around, sensing me and my seeking thread.

Here's where you can laugh at ol' Darcy.

I went to my knees.

Yes. Picture it. It's 10:30 at night, downtown Atlanta, on a busy stretch of clubs and bars, with dozens of mortals milling on all sides. And picture Avel, fucking beautiful, dark eyes, a half-Caucasian afro of tight ringlets—each moving as independent creatures with every movement of his head. His arm slipped away from his companion as he watched me go to my knees. He lowered his chin, considered me, my face bringing him incredible joy. The protocol demanded I greet him, but for one of the few times in my life, my tongue didn't work. I parted my lips, looking up at my master, my ass resting on my heels, and I couldn't say the words he needed to hear. But he was an Elder-Candidate—not an Elder and this is what saved the moment.

"Kolz's polsc'v' lz..."[17] he whispered in our language.

If I'd been mortal, I would have squeezed out tears. I offered a tiny nod and he put out both hands. Out of the corner of my eye, I watched his companion's mouth. She wanted his attention returned to her, but she was done. Avel moved away from her with drama and told her to fuck off, all the while holding my eye. I took his hands and he tugged until I stood.

Oh, dear reader, I had been thirsty for an Elder for *so long!* He was six feet tall, so I now looked upon him as he grinned at my height. He looked so young—all of us age slowly, and he was centuries old—you would have thought he was barely twenty-one. Elders find it easy to project an age they choose. I worked to appear no more than thirty, but I did not have the power to look younger. No matter, for the moment, I read in the Candidate's eyes that I was everything he ever wanted and more.

"Do you have a room?" he asked in our language and I smiled, finally able to speak.

"Master," I managed, "come home with me. I have

---

[17] "My perfect and matchless favored one/savior." (Rakum Hungarian)

a house. Barely ten miles away."

"I am Avel," he said and wove his arm in mine, indicating we should walk.

"Darcy Vandiver, Master," I said and led him across the busy street to my haphazardly parked pickup. I showed him into the passenger side and got behind the wheel. Ignoring angry drivers, I got us pointed toward my house down the road.

"Who was your last Elder, Darcy?" he asked and I loved his sweet voice, higher than mine, but with a gravel at the end of each word.

"Master Bel," I answered and glanced at him as often as was safe.

"Ah, Bel, he taught me much in my time with him. My time with Jack Dawn was more recent, and Elder Tomás at Last Assembly."

I nodded, and blinked, needing so desperately to get him to my house, my bed. Then he said something that only increased my excitement.

"You take my breath away," he whispered and then scooted across the bench seat to sit against me. His left hand landed on my thigh, open and kneading the muscle. "I haven't seen a fix-it man since 1799. His name was Jersey. Do you know him?"

I grinned and pressed the gas pedal to zoom the final mile to my driveway. "Oh, yes, Master. Jersey mentored me under Elder Kilmeade. We were compatible."

Avel laughed one huff and dropped his head to my shoulder, leaning against me like a mortal on a date. "Then you will be compatible with Avel. Jersey and I hit it off and he showed me some wonderful ishy things."

I grinned with a nod and whipped the truck into my drive. "Please, let's get inside. I see what you need, Master. I see it so clearly and I want so desperately to tend to it right now."

Avel smiled and allowed me to come around to get his door. He also allowed me to help him down with a hand to his bicep. He didn't need "help," but the contact and the subservience touched his need and that is what I lived for. I got him inside and without delay, I shuttled him to my light-tight sleeping quarters in my barricaded basement. I did not intend on being finished before dawn, so we may as well bunk down.

Avel watched me bolting the door and heard me doing the same upstairs using my superb telekinesis. He loosened his tie without pulling it off, unbuttoned the top button of his dress shirt and began removing items from his slacks pockets to set on my nightstand. When I turned to face him, squaring up but still twenty feet away, our eyes met and he held up his palm in a stop gesture.

"Slow your jets, Darcy. The fire in your eyes will consume me."

I waited a nanosecond to gauge his meaning; did he truly question my muse or was he making light of my saved-up exuberance? Maybe it was our entire race's loss of telepathic prowess since Last Assembly, but I could not read his meaning. I could, however, read my muse. The two of us had never been more connected and I followed its lead as I had since age 9 when Elder Pebb discovered me.

I zoomed into Avel's space, knocked his protest aside, grasped his face with both hands and pressed our mouths together. He kissed me back, Judas Priest! Did he reciprocate! But still, he cowered. I noted this but plowed on, following, trusting, and knowing that I was right. He could break down in tears right then, and I would still know I was right. Think back to my run-in with Father Damien. If the Father said I made an error, and then I countered and he bowed to my expertise, how much more so should an Elder-Candidate accept that Darcy Vandiver knew precisely how to bring satisfaction to his master?

"Darcy!" he said in a yelp, ripping his mouth away and tossing his face to one side.

We were still clothed, standing toe to toe. My warm palms had followed his movement for the first second, but I dropped them to his throat.

"Shh shh shh," I whispered so low he would need telepathy to hear me, and I touched my lips butter-soft to his forehead. Again, I sent and whispered for him to be quiet, be still, *"your servant has this well in hand..."*

Oh, muse, my muse, I love you...

My next move was a novel one. In three-hundred

years uncovering and attending my masters' needs and I was led to do something entirely new. If there had been any brethren present, oh, they would have gawked. Bending at the waist, I shot one arm behind Avel's knees and the other behind his shoulders and lifted him up until I held him before me like a giant child.

"Darcy, goddammit, put me the fuck down…"

There had been no fire, no anger in his voice, only the sound of a Rakum who understood he might be the last Elder. In his mind, that is akin to being the last Rakum, because they were so immensely superior to the balance of our people. Yes, he had never been officially graduated to the post, but he had completed the trials. He had been intimately tethered to all one hundred, more tightly than the rest of us could comprehend. After Last Assembly, their lines went down—like holding hands with a hundred people your entire life only to have them vanish in a blink. See? That is heavy. And in 2018, we did not know that there were any Elders left alive.

"Shut the fuck up, Master," I said in his ear using my voice to tickle him deep inside, carrying him to my bed.

I lay him longwise, his head to the pillows and leaned over him to look into his face. His expression was like I had never seen in a brother nor a master—the face said, *save me,* and you can bet I would succeed.

"My beautiful, beautiful lover, you will never know how wonderful you are to my eyes," I said, petting him with my words and my hands, taking time with every button. Tiny tugs to remove his shirt, gentle movements to remove his cotton undershirt and then those nutty tailored suit pants. Oh, he dressed for the ladies, this one, and I took care with his threads as I put them aside.

"Darcy," he said in a tiny voice, his eyes in mine, his expression morphing, joining the dance my song initiated.

Our threads lined up, intertwining in our mental spaces like the old days, before Last Assembly when the Rabbit and her God screwed up our lives. In my mind's eye, his silvery telepathic fiber wrapped itself fully around mine and Avel was a full goddamn Elder for that moment.

When we came up for air, three hours had passed, the sun was nearing the horizon and there was nothing to do but remain in bed.

At sundown, Avel was a different man and I would never see that look on his face again. Whatever psychological event accosted him before meeting me that night, me and my muse erased his trauma and saved him.

But didn't I name this chapter *The Sexpert Goes Human?* Here is why I told you all of that.

I saw Avel on the road seven days before the world went to shit. Each night following that first (rather bizarre) one, he and I hit the clubs, found beautiful people to fuck and drink and we ended a few before the week was up. Why not? As far as I was concerned, he was a Rakum Elder, the last one, and all mine.[18] If we drank someone to death, *whoops.* We hid the body. With a powerful Elder on your arm, so much more was possible than a grunt by himself, and we were lonely in those days, as I mentioned.

Here's where I explain in brief why he was still an Elder-Candidate in 2018. High Father Abroghia's edict from the beginning was only one hundred Elders were allowed at a time. Until one of our masters fell off his pedestal (ahem, perished), Avel remained a Candidate. He was a Rakum so he wouldn't complain aloud. Shit, before Last Assembly, he wouldn't complain to himself, since all of the Elders and Fathers could (and did) read him.

But in bed, underground, in the dark, and between the covers, little subconscious bits of disgruntlement seeped from his brainwaves. Being ishy, I picked it up and loved him all the more for it. How utterly mortal for a Rakum to whine. I loved it. He never admitted it, but he couldn't deny what I was intuiting. Fuck, my telepathy was supernatural when it came to fixing my masters, so Avel took my word for it: deep down, somewhere he would never look into, the Candidate wished one of the Hundred would die off. This was moot

---

[18] *Turns out, Avel wasn't the last Elder, but I didn't know any better at the time. Details are in "The Rabbit Saga" for those interested. ~ Darcy*

since our race had been scattered, but his regret ran deep.

Sundown the night we went mortal, Avel and I had been in bed awaiting time to exit the light tight room. Rakum can't bear the sunlight. More succinctly, our eyes can't. My skin would blister if exposed fifteen seconds. In sixty seconds, I would burn—but all the while, my skin would heal as it burned. I could get inside or undercover before I expired. The problem was our eyes. We could not stand even a single direct beam of ultraviolet light. A spear of UV would blind one of us for hours, so we were careful to remain below ground or under thick cover until the sun dipped below the horizon.

The Night of Shit (heh, I'm going to start calling it that), Avel had been giggling, silly and high, just happy to be with his favorite lay. I loved his laugh and I would joke and kid and tickle to make him laugh even louder. He'd been sleeping mostly with females the past few years and had not been able to find our brethren. I told him it's because they were hiding from him—if they sensed an Elder or a Candidate around, they would not want to be engaged. Our leaders had gone insane—the ones that remained—and I knew because I hid, too.

But, he had not lain with a brother since Last Assembly so when I took him to bed that first time, I veritably rocked his world more than he'd had in decades, maybe even since he was with Jersey. This night, the Night of Shit, he was breathless with laughing and we had not started the launch. I asked him about

Jersey.

"He was my first ish-mikhan and it's a wonder you never heard the tale of Jersey felling a Master," Avel said, smiling wide and collapsing on his back on my bed. He was shirtless, but still wearing blue jeans and socks. He folded his hands on his middle and watched me. I had ceased tickling him and was propped upon an elbow to see his face.

"He felled you? I don't understand."

Avel nodded with a new chuckle. "Master Dawn informed me that I would meet a ish-mikhan named Jersey and then he challenged me, saying, 'I bet you can't resist him.'" Avel's eyes flashed in mine at the thought. "I took that bet. I mean, how could a mere grunt overcome me?"

I grinned now realizing his error had been underestimating a fix-it man. It was a rookie mistake and I waited for more of the tale.

"A rookie, indeed," he said now able to read me much better since we had connected our bodies as well as minds. "Jack led me and the company into a receiving hall and that's when I first saw him. Fuck-me, I knew at a glance that if he looked at me hard, I'd fall apart. I had never seen such a specimen."

Avel's voice grew soft and he lifted a hand to my pecs. He stroked across my chest hair, eyes on his own fingers and he continued.

"Jack told me to resist him and that fucker threw at

me every ounce of his power. I not only was the first to look away, but I went to my knees, simultaneously coming as if I'd never had an orgasm in my life. It was hilarious to the brethren present, but to me? It was amazing. How did he do that? I wanted to know and when Jack sent him to tend to the others, I asked for another private audience."

I nodded in an absent manner, recalling with great affection my beloved, picturing what Avel described. "In private, he fixed you, eh? He saw the Elder in you," I said as a statement.

"Yes, that's what he said, too. He saw my potential, and he saw my need. Can you guess what it was that night?"

I nodded, well aware because I'm a fix-it man, too. "You wanted him to teach you how to resist the ish-mikhan."

Avel laughed with new glee and tugged on my neck until I draped my chest across his. "Yes, and he did, but I would never use it. If he were here right now, I'd never use it, and I sure as fuck would never use it on you."

He needed a new kiss and I leaned in, smiling into his face when we were so close. "It is still early, Master," I told him planning the evening. It was after midnight with five good hours of night remaining. "I will take you on a hunt."

But Avel shook his head and pulled our mouths together for a deeper kiss. We'd been in bed since sundown, rising only for a quick sandwich and then we returned to the covers. It was as if Avel wanted to make up for lost time the way he stayed in romance mode. I stayed, too, and when he was ready, I showed him a new move he enjoyed, his eyes as big as saucers at the end. Breathless with pure joy, Avel suddenly grew serious.

"Darcy," he said in a whisper, his left palm open to the center of my chest. His hand inched down to my navel and stopped. He looked into my face. "Darcy," he said again at the same volume.

"Yes, Master, say it. I will make it happen," I said actively working to read what he wouldn't say. Then it popped free and I saw in his mind that he wanted to touch me. I already shared with you how Elders keep themselves apart by receiving pleasure, not giving. Avel had been fucked since Last Assembly. Not by a brother, but by a man he enjoyed. I looked deeper and Avel's hand remained as it was.

"Can you see him?" he asked me in a softer voice than before. "Kelvin. His name was Kelvin."

I concentrated and caressed Avel's mental thread until the vision cleared. Kelvin was strong, slender, and Black with dreads and double tattoo sleeves. He rode Avel with affection and care for his enjoyment of the lovemaking.

I refocused in Avel's gaze. "I can love you like Kelvin did, Master," I told him in my silky voice. "Would you like that?"

Avel nodded and I sensed admitting to another Rakum that he sometimes wanted to bottom caused him immense stress. I would tell him that the Elders are gone and he should do what pleases him. Then I told him a fact he could not dispute.

"Master Avel, who the fuck ever told a Rakum Elder what to do?"

Oh, he liked that. He liked that I thought of him as a full Elder. With his enthusiastic permission, I resumed our kiss, my hand snaking around to prepare him for the show. Imagine what was happening in Darcy Vandiver's heart and mind! I was about to make love to an Elder (and we've established I thought of him as full!). For the first time in my life, I would enter one of these amazing beings bred to be better, stronger, smarter, and all around more awesome then every other grunt. We kissed and moaned and just as I prepared to rock us both, the world turned upside down.

What does it feel like to "turn mortal"?

You've been to an amusement park, right? You board the roller coaster and ride up the first big hill. At the top, the brakes come off and you fly back to earth at speed, your stomach floats to your throat and your head swims—this is what it felt like.

Except it didn't end for several minutes.

And it happened to Avel, multiplied by ten because of his pre-Elder status.

We both collapsed to our backs on the huge bed,

both of us squeezing our eyes closed and moaning from deep down. Then, like synchronized swimmers, we both flipped to our opposite sides to vomit off the side of the bed.

When nothing heaved out except viscous liquid, I flopped back onto my back and dropped a hand to Avel's shoulder blades, him still leaned over the mattress.

"O'lz fah-fah," (I am here, I am here) I whispered in our language and with gentle strokes, I worked to comfort my newest friend. Minutes passed and he remained that way. Eventually, I sat up and wiped my face with my free hand, continuing to rub his smooth skin.

"Avel," I whispered, *"We're mortal."*

The words were horrible, but I knew to my bones it had happened. Over the past few years, I had heard of brethren who turned human voluntarily, who decided to relinquish their Rakum identity to be part of the Maker's world. I never wanted that. I didn't want to change; I didn't want to be like them—weak, hopeless, and disgusting.

But now we were.

Avel said nothing. He moved to a sitting position, slow and with effort, and put his feet to the floor, facing the opposite way.

"Avel, Master... I'm here," I said, sensing his distress despite having just lost a major portion of my muse.

He stood, still without speaking, and pulled on his trousers. That done, he shrugged on his dress shirt, disregarding that he'd worn an undershirt with it earlier. He did not look at me and I called his name again.

"It's going to be okay," I said not planning my words. "We'll figure it out. Avel?"

The Elder-Candidate affixed his gold tie and pushed sockless feet into his dress shoes, all without speaking or looking my way. He stepped toward the room door.

"Avel…" I got up and walked toward him. In response, he spun around, his eyes full of rage, which I read clearly even while losing every vestige of our birthright.

"Get. The FUCK! Back," he hissed, meaning every syllable.

I did as he commanded and stumbled backward until my ass met the mattress. He proceeded out and down the hall out of sight. I listened as he left, slamming the front door with gusto. Then I heard his Mercedes peel out of my driveway.

Shi-i-i-i-i-i-t.

Ask a person what it feels like to die and have to walk around as a ghost.

This is what we became.

For a time, I was angry. I stayed in a few nights, still unable to go into the sun, but within a month, UV light barely bothered me. I still had my Rakum brain so

132

I sought constant stimulation. I'm not proud of it now, but over the course of my transformative period, I raped and tortured more people than I can number.

Jersey wrote a book about how this Rakum fury affected my brothers, so be sure to check it out. It's called *Malcontent,* and I'm in there. I did what I could to help my frustrated brethren once I became accustomed to my new state of being.

A human being.

Like you.

And…

I lived on, I found balance, and I'm happy.

Read on to see what fun a vampire sexpert can have even when he's mortal. Turns out my cock works better than ever. Heh-heh.

10

My Straight CEO:

Round One

MY CEO BECAME ONE OF MY FAVORITE
MORTALS in recent years. For this reason, he earned a
place of honor in my vampire memoir—even though I
met him only after we'd lost our Rakum-ness. When we
went mortal, I used my Rakum inheritance (details
described in the Rabbit Saga) to purchase a construction
company and a fantastic executive home in Atlanta,
Georgia. My professional (human) name became Darcy

Pebb.[19] My company, Pebb Construction, grew into a multi-million-dollar enterprise in a very short time. Enter my CEO.

We shall call him Chief. Our adventure began when Chief's final job interview coincided with an invitation to visit a brother named Winston. Readers of the Saga would recognize his name—he's obsessed with me. I enjoy his adoration and he is extremely thankful in bed. When he asked if I'd enjoy a few days in his town, the idea tickled my spirit.

"Look, Darss," Winston said when he called, "Seven of our brothers meet here once a month for cards, whoring, whatever. We drink, we laugh, we go to the fight club, we have fun. Two of the brethren know you from your days with Elder Pebb..."

"Names," I said as I am always interested in reuniting with brothers I knew in the past.

"It's Tarn and Gilmore." Win chuckled as if with a memory. "Last month, the subject came around to the fix-it men. As you can imagine, I bragged on you straightaway and these two went nuts. They were pitiful." Win barked a few chuckles. "They said if I call you, I should say, *polz k'zak infay.*" (A literal translation is impossible, but if you imagine three men making love

---

[19] *How's that for an homage to my last master? Big secret reveal: when we assume human names, we often add our master's name to our own. Consider Emil Jersey – Jersey's first master was Elder Emil. There you go.*
~ Darcy

to each other at the same time, you'll be close.)

"When do I need to be there?" I said, ready to say yes.

Winston railed off the deets and was gone. My new CEO arrived for his last interview and I prepared to invite him along.

He sat in the wide office Queen Anne as if he owned the room. I liked that, knees slack and apart, elbows on the armrests with hands dangling without tension, and his head to the side. He was an alpha male and his resume paired with his persona said he could carry this company to higher heights.

I stood up from around my desk. He stepped toward me, hand out to shake. His grip was firm, his hand not as big as mine, but he matched the measure of muscle I used in every man-to-man handshake. "I have an inkling you might be the CEO this company needs for a long time."

Chief nodded. "I can say with all sincerity—if possible, I'd stay with Pebb till retirement."

He had answered perfectly. "I want you to come with me on a little trip next weekend. Think of it as the owner of this company wants a little bonding time. What do you say?"

I surprised him, his brows arched, but he recovered and chuckled. It was a good look for him, half-smile in that serious George Clooney face. I should mention, he doesn't actually resemble the actor, but he has that sort of swagger with an embrace of natural handsomeness.

"Just tell me what to pack," he said and gave my hand another firm pump. My trip to New York had become much more interesting.

On the flight from Atlanta to LaGuardia, Chief (I'm withholding his name) answered probing questions about his life. I knew he was divorced with three children in college, but I asked a new question to provoke him. I enjoy that.

"Do you sleep with guys?"

He wasn't offended. I've been on the planet long enough that I expect one of two reactions to that question. Chief had the right one.

"Not so far," he said with a chuckle that expressed he wasn't attracted to men but didn't want to offend his new boss if he happened to be. Smart.

I gave him a nod and leaned back to relax into the seat. "Tonight, we're invited to a private party. All men, and some of them might come on to you. These guys are family to me and mean no harm. All you have to do is say no."

"No problem," Chief said with a tip of his chin. He looked out the window on his side so I watched his profile as he continued. "I have some cousins who are gay and Sarah's first husband left her for a man." One shoulder made the tiniest shrug. "I guess you'd say when my personality and sex drive were being formed, I had no one in that vein to model after. I made myself into the image of my father. He was a great man and I have always wanted to be like him."

I made a tiny huff and he looked over, brows up. "What you just said sounds like a Bible verse," I told him with a wave of my hand. "I didn't ask before, but are you religious?"

"Does it matter?" he asked and I realized he meant as an employee.

"No, you have the job, even if you're a nutcase Republican Conservative Fundamentalist Christian," I responded with a half-smile.

He returned a full grin and rest his hands in his lap, relaxed as usual. "Guilty." He laughed then and watched my face. I suppose my expression caused him to think I was unsure of him now because he added, "I promise not to spread Gospel tracts around the construction site. On my honor."

I laughed and told him that was smart thinking. The car was pulling up to the hotel entrance and Chief reached to the floorboard for his briefcase. When he was sitting upright again, our eyes locked.

"If you don't believe in God, that's not my business," he said without a hint of judgment in his tone. The driver opened the door as he shot me one more glance to end with, "the Puppeteer will have his way with us no matter what we think or say or do." And he stepped onto the sidewalk.

The Puppeteer. Why would he call the God of the

mortals The Puppeteer? You see, Master Canaan used that term for the Maker the last few times I saw him. To hear this erudite and successful alpha use that same term... That was when Chief went on my NTF list. And I put an asterisk by his name—make it this weekend.

Winston had purchased a ranch house on eleven acres and he sent a car to pick us up at the hotel after we had showered and had a bite to eat. Chief was fifty and so far, he seemed fit enough to hang all night with a posse of former bloodsuckers. Speaking of fitness, I had arranged for us to have adjoining rooms. Once we had checked in and gone to our respective heads to piss, he rapped on the door between our rooms and said we should keep it open. I don't know if any of Jersey's readers get what that says to an ish-mikhan. Do they know what it says to a mortal boss man who holds the man's job in his sweaty palms? Multiply that by a factor of ten. Chief wanted me to come on to him. Did he want to fuck? No, the invitation didn't say that, but it said he expected, or at least would not be offended, if his new boss ogled him. Trust me. I've been doing this for centuries.

So we had the door ajar and with me in my room and him in his, we cleaned up and groomed for a night out. I was dressed in bootcut jeans and a deep red pullover, ready to go in twenty minutes, and he stepped into the opening between the two rooms wearing old-man boxers.

"Oh, good," he said with a glance at my outfit. Then he turned away saying, "I didn't want us to be twins."

Fifty-years old and he looked really good. He had no abdomen definition, probably lost that when he stopped lifting weights, but at some point in his past he lifted a lot. The round and wide shoulders I noticed through his clothing were thick with muscle trained over decades. Biceps not cut, but bulging and pecs as perfectly formed as my own, only not hard as they must have been during his gym days. None of that reduced my desire, no, my *need* to run my hand across his chest.

Shortly thereafter, Chief led the way to the elevator. He'd worn jeans, relaxed and worn-in, with work boots and a plaid shirt open two buttons. He looked like a CEO trying to look casual, and the funny thing? He was *trying* to look that way. He was playing a role for my brothers. I told him so in the elevator and he owned up.

"Yeah, I want to project exactly that—a stuffy businessman out for beers with the boss. A little nervous, a little unsure about the men he doesn't know, but hoping his overall performance impresses."

I got a really good laugh from that and clapped his shoulder. I gave him a word of advice before the door opened to the lobby. "For the rest of this trip, do not refer to The Puppeteer by that name," I said grinning and he matched my expression. "A very passionate part of my past used that term and when you say it, I get hard in all the right places. *Comprende?"*

140

I had used Elder Canaan's word, too, and actually did make my jeans a little snug. Chief nodded holding my eye. He believed me and he comprehended. I let it drop—if he got too close, he would be fucking Darcy Vandiver. As far as I am concerned, I warned him. His new boss likes men and may have taken a shine to his new CEO.

It took thirty minutes to reach Win's estate and Chief and I swapped war stories. I'd been playing with mortals long before we lost our mojo, as Jersey calls it, so I know how to turn my actual experiences into tales fit for human ears. Once the car stopped at an impressive two-story Ranch home, we got out without the driver's assistance and headed up the walk. I had sent to Win's phone, *"+1 Pulgh osc'l'v"* (a mortal unaware of Rakum), so I wasn't surprised no one met us in the yard. They were probably inside planning how to act around Darcy Vandiver and now a mortal who knew nothing of their people.

I grinned as I pushed open the door—this was precisely why I brought my CEO as a buffer.

"Kazak!" Tarn belted and jogged to meet me in the doorway. I hadn't even stepped across the threshold before he shouldered Chief aside and grabbed my neck. The squirt came up to my chin and to chap his ass I resisted his tug. He was in my eye and read I was being an asshole. He grinned and kissed what he could reach.

I moved him to my right and held him in place with

an arm about his shoulders. I hadn't seen him since Assembly 1950, but it felt as if only a day had passed, so familiar we were. I positioned myself next to Chief and flopped my left arm on him the same way and faced the men looking at us from the main room.

"Kazak, brothers," I announced and then I said in Rakum Hungarian, "just use our language on private stuff." I introduced Chief for who he was and all the guys came forward. Gilmore, my other Pebb bunkmate came close and Chief had stepped away to shake hands and make greetings. Being alone a moment, my old pal got the kiss he deserved and told me I looked better than ever.

The four brothers I hadn't met circled up and Tarn, Gilmore and Winston stayed back, engaging Chief in chatter. These guys were all from Fawn's pack and knew Winston since First Ritual. I won't belabor their descriptions because I can sum them up in one word: hungry. They had been soldiers in the Old Way, and they filled their nights with violence and blood. They mostly fucked each other and had no finesse with women. I read in their faces that being mortal hadn't lessened their Rakum drive for chaos and destruction. Once each man made small flirtations to me, complimenting me in whatever way they could imagine, they opened the ring for me to go into the big room.

Winston came up and waited for me to turn. "You look well," he said low after a new kazak. "You're the guest of honor so what will it be?" His eyes flit to Chief and back.

Chief looked over from his conversation with Tarn. I sent him a wink that said it's not important and he turned back.

"We have a few great clubs, a brothel, and right here a card game with all the booze, weed, and conversation you need."

Win had given me the choices holding my eye. In the old days, I would have read his thoughts, but his eyes begged enough.

"The others have kissed me quite a lot in front of my straight CEO," I told him in Rakum Hungarian very low. "Now you want to kiss the fix-it man, too?" Win's mouth made the tiniest grin. He wanted much more than a kiss.

The feeling and thought that hit me at that moment is the only reason I considered avoiding Win since the Last Battle.[20] I wanted to turn back time, grab that asshole and yank him to the bedroom. Why? In a very short minute, we'd be done and the entire night lay ahead. What came from such an insignificant explosion of sensation? As a Rakum, we had no use for a clock. We avoided the sun but the rest of the minutes worked for us, not against. I would do the man, do maybe Tarn and Gilmore, and watch the others jerk each other off and we'd go find some Cows and drink as much blood as

---

[20] This is what we call the night we all turned mortal. ~ Darcy

possible. All without a care. Now? I only wanted to see what Chief would do if presented with the opportunity to fuck his boss.

I checked my CEO's position and he was facing away, still talking with the others, and I gave Winston more kiss than he deserved. When I released him, he tugged his jeans at the crotch and excused himself.

To the room I announced, "Chief and I want to play cards. Set 'em up." I took my place beside my employee and we sat together at the table. I focused my attention on him over the next three hours of cards and drinks. Neither he nor I smoked or imbibed in narcotics, but a few of my brothers let loose and eventually came to blows, fussing over something stupid.

At 2 AM, Winston asked me privately to sleep over. I considered it—well, I considered slipping upstairs with him a few minutes and returning to take Chief back to the hotel. But then I'd smell like Winston—some cheap ass cologne that I did not care for. I told him in his ear, "I want to try out the Chief so I'll come by tomorrow night." I watched his eyes and he nodded, enjoying my consideration. In another few minutes, I led Chief to the door and he went to the car when I said I needed a moment to say goodbye.

Tarn and Gilmore kissed me too long, but I was behind the door, not wanting Chief to see too much of that stuff. Once I was in the car with him, we headed back and he didn't speak for a full minute. I didn't care,

I had nothing to say, buzzing pleasantly on the last two shots of bourbon I'd nabbed before the goodbyes began. Chief still sat front-and-center on the F-list, but I could imagine falling asleep instead. Sometimes that happens now that I'm mortal—a urge to snooze can overshadow a bang if the circumstances are right.

"The High Father didn't do that," Chief said in a low voice, not speaking to me, but to the air. That combination of words didn't fit in a human's mouth and my ears perked. Chief repeated the phrase the same way, still looking out the window. One of my brothers must have said that in his hearing, but how could it matter?

Chief and I sat across from each other in the stretch limo and I kicked both legs out to the center to slump downward in the soft leather. Draping my arms across the back of the bench seat, I watched his profile. I know enough about human behavior to realize when a man mumbles in that fashion, he's not seeking a query. He was drunk and repeating an odd phrase that for some reason stuck in his head.

"I'd kill the Rabbit if I ever saw her," he said in the same voice, but this time as he reached the word "saw" he turned his face to mine. "I'd kill the Rabbit," he said again, now seeking my response. "Does that mean anything to you?"

I didn't reply, but watched his eyes, vainly trying to divine his thoughts on the matter. Why would he ask unless the phrase meant something to him?

"What does it mean to you?" I ask, eyebrows up, as innocent as a lamb.

Chief exhaled a long breath and shrugged, end of topic. He looked back out the window. "Your friends were sure different."

I chuckled but he didn't turn. "Tell me about it," I said agreeing.

"I needed a Babblefish in my ear." Chief was leaning on the right side of the car and he swiveled his chin, his body still sideways. "The more they drank, the more they spoke in that top-secret language of yours." He said the last part with humor and shimmied his body to a more upright position. Out the windshield, I saw the hotel sign; we were pulling up.

"We speak at least four languages, my brothers and I," I said and closed my mouth. What the shit? I was comfortable, a little floaty from the booze, but I had spoken too close to the line. I tried to cover it with a follow-up. "How about you, Chief? Your resume said you speak English and Spanish. Any other linguistics in your lineup?"

"Does pig-Latin count?" he asked with a grin.

The limousine stopped and the driver's shape approached the tinted window. Chief exited first and I followed, neither speaking until we had hit the lobby elevator bank.

I hit our floor and the car started up before Chief said with a new smile, "You tired?"

146

I grinned with interest. "What do you have in mind?"

Chief nodded and when the door opened, he walked out, a little come-hear-finger wiggling over his shoulder as he left. I followed, still smiling and wondering what he was thinking. Nothing that transpired the past thirty minutes was the least bit sexual, so I worked every other possible angle. Had it to do with languages? Killing Rabbits? High Fathers? When we reached our pair of rooms, he opened his door and led me inside.

"Have a seat," he said with a knuckle to the long hotel couch. I was game and dropped into it longways, propping my feet on the other end as he disappeared into the bedroom. He returned almost immediately with a book and he dropped it in my lap as he passed to sit in the adjacent matching chair.

The Rabbit, by Beth Rider-Stone.[2] *Shit.* Do Jersey's readers know what that is? In short, it's a book about what happened to a woman named Beth Rider when she was marked as a Rabbit by Master Dawn. I was not involved in that fuck-up, but I read the book. Maybe this is where I admit, like the Rabbit, I believe in the Maker.

At any rate, back to Chief handing me this novel. You'd be surprised at my reaction. I forced a languid gaze and played dumb. "You want me to read this?"

"That's what they were talking about," he said making himself comfortable. He crossed one ankle over his knee, elbows on the armrests, his hands loose in his lap. He tilted his chin right as he watched for my reaction. It was a good look for him, authoritative, in charge, cocksure. I remembered my F-list.

"They? My brothers?" I asked and might have flinched. Mortals don't talk like that unless they're in a cult. He showed a grin that said, *ah-hah!*. I still played dumb, no longer tipsy and wanting to be.

"You don't want to talk about it?" he asked with another vague gesture to the book in my hand.

"I'm not in this book," I said teasing and tossed it to him eight feet away. "Say what's on your mind." He sat up enough that it dawned on me we were going to talk for hours. There'd be no fucking and I was deciding if that worked for me.

"I think this book is true and you and all those men tonight are part of this secret race of vampires." Chief did not crack a smile even though his words must have sounded strange to his own ears. Humans don't believe in vampires, why would he think the book is true? I asked him and he said, "if one plus one is two, it's true whether I believe it or not."

I pursed my lips and watched his eyes. He did not waver. "Bring every bottle of booze you have in that minibar," I said in a commanding voice,

Chief offered a victorious wink and rose to comply. He returned with eleven minis carried in his newly un-tucked dress shirt. He allowed them to drop across my lap and I watched the three inches of his fuzzy belly until

148

he stepped away. He returned to his chair but with both hands, yanked the heavy furniture closer so we were half the distance apart. I remained reclined across the sofa and tossed him a Svedka.

"I'm not admitting anything, but I'll turn anything into a drinking game." I grabbed my own mini and held it up, sealed. "If you ask a question, you down a mini. Same for me. Answers can be true or false, but must make sense. When the booze is gone, the game is done."

Chief grinned and lifted his upper body to peek in my lap. "Someone gets an extra question."

I waggled my eyebrows. "That's part of the fun."

"I'll go first," he said and gurgled down his vodka. I chuckled when he choked on the final drop. "Went down the wrong pipe," he managed and cleared his throat several times with hilarious facial expression until he could speak again. "Okay... you can lie so let me make it a good one..."

He had specific questions. What was happening? I wasn't about to reveal myself with this fantastic new CEO who would serve to bring me more money than ever. While he worked his questions into the proper form, I prepared my cult responses. I did not want the man to go away thinking the owner of Pebb Construction spent three centuries as a vampire.

"Okay, boss-man," he said with snark, a watery sparkle in his deep blue eyes after the quick shot, "You said you aren't in this book, which means you recognize it, so my question is, explain to me why you said you aren't in it."

I smiled—he worked hard to formulate a question that yes or no wouldn't serve. Plus, there was a little mind-fuck going on between us. He was sitting forward now, leaning over his knees, and I read something hungry in his eye. Not for sex, but something… Part of my mind worked that issue while I began my answer.

"I read that book two years ago when recommended by a colleague. I recognized your Rabbit and High Father phrases from the novel when we were in the car. When we discussed it later, I felt like being a little roguish, pretending I was part of another race." I held his gaze the entire time and slowly sat up to match his posture, leaning forward over my knees with my hands dangling. I'm five inches taller and at least seventy pounds heavier, but we must have looked like a nice pair, facing off like that. "I mean, I have the look. I could be a vampire, right?"

Chief almost answered and smiled. "Is that your question?"

"Is that your second question?" I said with cheek.

"Only if that's yours."

He was quick-minded. I rolled in my bottom lip and held it with my teeth, watching his eyes still. His gaze flit to my mouth and my chin and lower before he looked back. He was straight, but I'm very beautiful. With my teeth I unscrewed my mini and downed it holding his attention. "That's my question. I know I look like one of those vampires in the book. Am I beautiful? What does my CEO think? Go ahead."

He remained forward but blushed as the moments passed. He smiled to the side. "I can lie, remember?" I nodded. "Boss-man," he repeated and I snickered. "You look like a vampire, all right. You look like a devil. I'm fifty years old, dedicated to my children and my career, I go to church on the holidays and pray when I'm in trouble, but you get me alone and *shit...* I could forget myself. I think you're not human. Or you used to be something else. If this book is true, you could be a fallen angel in the flesh." He laughed and prepared another mini to shoot. "Satisfied?" he asked, the bottle poised by his lips.

I gave him a slow nod and he knocked it back. In five seconds, he exhaled and pound his sternum once. "Ooh, I should stick to beer." I waited for him to ask something, floating on his compliments. They had been vague, but he meant them. When he parted his lips to speak, I made a big show of opening my shirt half-way down. I don't shave my chest and he laughed when I stroked over my own pecs. "Your question?" I said with a flat expression.

"Your brothers," he said in finger quotes, "don't look like you. They're all fine-looking guys, but you look like a sex doll." He laughed at his own words. "I discern—and maybe it's the vodka speaking—but I discern you might have been an expert in seduction when you lived the old way."

"The old way," I repeated.

He was too close to knowing the truth, but it was a game, right? In the morning, we would both pretend the entire thing was farce. Right?

"Is that the question?" I asked and got to my feet. I took one step nearer and he leaned back, craning his face to mine. "In this pretend world of vampires and Rabbits and High Fathers, was your new boss a Sexpert?" I asked with a grin and licked my lips in slow motion. He had said he could forget himself. Had I heard that right?

"Is it pretend?" he asked in a softer, cautious voice. I took another step near, now an arm's length away and as he was seated his chin was at my belt-level.

"Everything is pretend when you're away from home, drinking with a god at 2 AM," I replied in my bedroom voice. Without planning to, I had fallen into seduction mode. The poor guy. He didn't have a chance.

"Ah-hah," he said weakly. "That's what they said in the book. They believed they were gods until they met the real God…"

He remained seated, looking up at me, and I moved a careful palm to his cheek. He hadn't shaved since the night before and I feathered my hand across the new growth. "Whose turn is it?" I asked in a whisper meant to send chills to his flesh and it worked.

"Yours," he said, only moving his lips.

I reached for a mini he held in his hand and for that two seconds, our faces were inches apart. I made certain to meet his eye up close and then stood. I sucked it down, wiped my chin with an exaggerated movement, and tossed the plastic container over my shoulder. I bent enough to grasp his right bicep and tugged until he gained his feet. I didn't need Rakum hearing to know his heart pounded when he stood facing me, less than two feet from chest to chest.

"My question goes like this," I said very softly and watching his mouth. *"Have you ever kissed a god?"*

Chief hadn't kissed a god, hadn't kissed a man. He hadn't wanted to. White-bread, all-American, muscular, Judeo-Christian life, he didn't take drugs or abuse women. He didn't watch porn and hadn't stolen anything more than a pack of gum. But I tell you right now, dear reader, he was aching to kiss the fix-it man.

This is where my expertise comes in. He had no words and I don't know what he would have said if I didn't do my part next. I cupped his face with my palms and Chief's body responded—no need for human labels of gay or bi or straight. At that instant, we were compatible, and I lowered to touch our lips. He did not return anything as I molded my mouth to his, gentle, quiet, allowing our breath to intermingle. He received me, but not fully. Not yet. I moved my palms to his neck, cradling the base of his skull. I'm huge and when a person feels my size on them, they dissolve. Chief was alpha, but he was also human. A sexual being lived inside the CEO and when three long seconds passed, our mouths touching and my hands so gentle around his head, he exhaled, and I moved in.

Once our tongues were dancing, two beautiful men began to undress. When I got him to the bed, he hadn't explored my body, rather he encompassed my forearms with his fingers. We were down to our boxers, kissing deeper and both aroused, and I had him sit on the edge of the bed. My eyes drank in his every inch, but he only stared at my face. This was new to me. Even straight men, when seduced by the fix-it man, mimic what is performed on their person. Chief didn't reach out. His eyes flicked down when I slid off my final garment, but he hadn't yet volunteered contact. When I reached for his hand to place it on my chest, he held it there unmoving, looking into my face. Part of him was petrified but an equal part was already fucking a man for the first time. Another long moment passed with his palm encompassing my right breast, in place but not moving, and I made up my mind.

One gentle push to his shoulder and he lay back, looking up at me as if I was a giant and he was a child. Completely out of character, I whispered, "Do you want me to leave?"

"No," he croaked and said more firmly, "No. Lie down." I gave him a small grin and lay alongside. I started the show and he said in my ear very small, *"The*

Puppeteer is watching…"

I told Chief to shut-it and he said nothing else. I'm a work in progress and the Maker knows it better than anyone. The CEO and the Boss-man wrestled until they fell asleep, in the same bed like an old married couple. In the morning, Chief left as I showered. He took a cab to the airport and hired a new flight. He left me a note, which I'll share here by permission.

Boss-man, I enjoyed our bonding adventure, and I look forward to bringing Pebb Construction to higher and higher levels over the next several quarters. Maybe I'll see you at the Christmas Party in Cancun. Bam-bam said it is always a huge hit and drinking games are encouraged. Kazak! ~ (name redacted)

So, there you go. Chief is still my CEO and I will seek him out at the party. I always have plenty of minis in my luggage.

11

My Straight CEO:

Round Two / Rendezvous

CHIEF HAD BEEN WITH PEBB CONSTRUCTION NINE MONTHS when our annual company trip came around. At this time, I was barely a year into my humanness and still quite mischievous. I had in my mind that I'd take him on round two. We hadn't had any reason to make contact since our drinking game and I looked forward to reading his expression when I pop into the meeting.

The Board of Directors had assembled at Pebb headquarters, the idea being to have one last planning meeting before putting away the shovel and the hardhat. I demanded that no work would be done in Cancun, so this is why I allowed a final business powwow.

Everyone had arrived, settled in the conference room down the hall from my office, and I waited for my moment. I would enter the room when I could garner the most attention. I'm mortal now, but old habits die hard (if at all).

The conference room walls are glass so anyone in the hallway can view inside. I planned to walk the long route so my board would see my beauty and have a moment to ponder everything that is Darcy Vandiver before I reached the door. I had almost reached the first glassed panel when my phone rang. It was Jersey so I answered, casually stepping into view of my board, eleven men and women around a long table, faces to the head where Chief led the conversation. I waited for any of them to notice me standing in the hall with my phone to my ear. Chief was the first to look up. His eyes widened, and then... yes, there it was. He smiled, blushed, and got to his feet. The rest of the board turned to look and give me nods and waves. I offered a general half-grin and leaned against the opposite wall facing them, crossing my feet and arms, still on the phone with Jersey. I was the picture of perfection and read that in every eye. It didn't matter the watcher's age, sex, race, or religion—I had (so far) retained my appeal.

I enjoyed those long gazes, especially that of the one or two already wondering what I might be like in bed.

Chief knew firsthand and he was red as a beet. I did not look at him, hoping to save him some measure of embarrassment as I finished up my call. Then my phone was in my pocket and I headed into the room.

Chief yanked open the glass door before I could do so myself. "Mr. Pebb, good to see you again," he said working to sound normal and hide from the group that he'd fucked the boss. He made a wide berth and returned to his chair.

I nodded to the faces and Chief introduced the ones I hadn't met. Each member had thanked me for the vacation and when they fell still I asked them all to sit. Chief was listening like a CEO should, but he didn't need to keep looking at me. I want to sleep with him again, so to preserve his secret, I crossed to stand behind his chair and face the others.

"It is 12:58," I said and put my hands to Chief's shoulders from behind. "When will you conclude this business?" I asked with a tiny movement in my hands so Chief would know he was addressed.

Looking forward, he cleared his throat. "All we need is five more minutes."

I gave his shoulders another small squeeze. "Excellent. When this meeting is done, your vacation begins and I would be unhappy to learn any of you did any work for the next seven days. Comprende?" I used Canaan's word and readers familiar with my people understand what that means. I was making myself hard and I chuckled before adding for the group, "Accounting has deposited five thousand dollars into each of your accounts to use for cash and I insist you use your Pebb c-card for any purchases upward of ten grand. This is a personal gift from me to you. Who knows what all this means?"

I finished and met the eyes. They appreciated my generosity and were surprised at the numbers, but no one spoke. With my hands open on Chief's outer shoulders, I allowed both thumbs to run across his skin out of sight of the others. He piped in with an answer.

"Mr. Pebb wants us to *not* work and *not* spend our own money on this vacation," he said.

"That's right," I agreed and added, "the jets are on the runway." I paused to meet the eyes of the senior Vice President of Sales, a woman I had met before but not bedded. When she averted her eyes in a demure blush, I continued. "Keep in mind the villas in this resort belong to the company. Kiki has assign you rooms, but swap around any way you like. This trip is about fun and some of you wish to know me better, yes?" I asked and all of them agreed with varying responses. I leveled my gaze with seriousness. "Everything your boss does outside of his suites is open to your company. When I am in view, come see me. I want to know you, too."

Under my palms, Chief huffed a laugh and I gave him a little massage no one else would see.

"Okay, ladies and gentlemen, finish this shit and

let's go to Cancun," I said and dropped the contact with my CEO. I headed for the door to close with, "and on my private beaches, swimsuits optional."

I walked out, going the long way down the hall so they could watch me leave. Kiki jogged up as I reached reception and handed over an envelope of cash that I had requested. She wanted to speak but took too long to gather the courage. I do not want to sleep with her again and she senses it, but this doesn't keep her from dreaming.

I headed for the elevator. Inside a young man worked the panel and Kiki hadn't found her words.

"Get to the airport," I told her only allowing a momentary eye meet. "Your vacation has begun." She parted her lips but said nothing as the doors closed in her face. "Garage," I said without looking at the youth and he pressed the key.

In another moment, he cleared his throat. "Pardon me, but are you Mr. Pebb?"

I turned to see the youth. This boy was beautiful. Soft, pink, maybe 5'9", but sturdy with his adolescent shoulders square and serious. His cheeks were smooth and his lips full and ruddy, and his blue-green eyes asked other questions that I knew his mouth would never utter. I raised my eyebrows combined with a small nod.

"Oh, good, I mean," he said with a stumble, as if he hadn't planned anything more than his opener. "Harry said you were. I just didn't believe it."

The elevator had reached the garage and he allowed

160

the door to open. "Your floor, sir." I had held his gaze this whole time and didn't release.

"Why didn't you believe him?" I asked with a tilt to my chin. Shit, you caught me, I was in seduction mode with the baby of the elevator car world.

His pale cheeks reddened as he answered. "Oh, because I guess I thought you were an actor or something. Maybe a prince." He nodded and pressed his lips together.

"How old are you?" I asked, aware that as a Rakum I'd have heard his heart hammer in his chest.

"Twenty-one, sir," he said, but he was lying. I studied mortals for three centuries—you can't lie around me. I'll see it. So when I only stared at him, he corrected. "I'm eighteen."

"Why the lie?" I asked, indicating he should close the door with us inside. He did so.

"I'm sorry, I didn't mean to. Honest. The job application said I had to be twenty-one."

His expression had dropped and I stepped close enough to press the PrV key in the top right of the panel. He watched my action, recoiling an inch until I returned to my place.

"What does that do?" he asked.

"Pauses the car for a private conversation. All of my elevators have this function. Tell me about yourself. What is your name?"

"Oh! I'm sorry," he stuttered. "I'm Sheamus. Very nice to meet you, Mr. Pebb." And he put out his hand.

I shook it and then without releasing, I turned his hand over in mine and clasped it between my palms. He didn't pull away, but watched for my next comment or question with trusting eyes.

"And who is Harry?" I asked, reading his pulse with my fingertips at his wrist.

"Oh," Sheamus said and blushed deeper than before. "He's a friend. He works in the mailroom."

The boy shrugged his right shoulder downward, indicating distress. I held his eye to give him a calming diversion. Very slowly, I ran my tongue across my lips and his pulse slowed to a normal beat, his nervous perspiration ceasing. Now, I would dig out his worry.

"Friends don't hurt each other," I said in my silkiest voice. "How does Harry hurt you?"

"Oh, he doesn't," the boy said on reflex but took it back still in my eye. "I mean, it doesn't matter. He doesn't mean anything by it. We're friends. He's my *boyfriend.*"

He had whispered the word and I had already sensed much of what he wouldn't say. As I had done a hundred times before, I cursed the universe that I was no longer Rakum. I'd have read this boy, he was open, pure, no malice, no malcontent, just a baby really, swimming with sharks. I watched his face another long moment, he was incapable of saying the words, incapable of admitting aloud that mailroom Harry sexually assaulted him, and cruelly, by the body language cues Sheamus put off.

"Is Harry working right now?" I asked and with a

162

boyfriend's loyalty, Sheamus pulled free of my grasp and shook his head.

"Yeah, but what? Are you going to fire him? Really, I don't know what you're thinking, Mr. Pebb, but don't fire him. He needs this job."

I put a finger to his lips and he hushed, the way he fell into my gaze so much like they did before 11/13. But I didn't count on it. I remembered I am mortal.

"Take me to the mailroom. That is an order," I added at the end and the obedient kid's mouth made a grim line as he pressed the button. Once there, the doors opened and I touched his cheek, aware that anyone in the mailroom would see. Next, in a seamless movement of two thumbs, I sent HR a message, then said to Sheamus, "Go see my receptionist. You've been promoted, and don't worry about Harry. I'm not firing him today."

With a stiff nod, he looked past me to someone across the room and the doors closed with a whisper. I smiled and turned to my employees.

"Harry?" I said aloud and of the seven men and women pausing in their sorting, only one did not look away.

"Yes, sir?" the man furthest into the dungeon space answered. This one was six feet, but soft with pockmarked cheeks and a sparse mustache.

"Follow me," I told him, turning in a smooth movement, headed for a maintenance door at the end of the hall.

He followed four strides behind and when I reached my goal I opened the door and entered, flipping the light switch as I passed. The tiny storeroom floor was only ten by ten, so when the boyfriend entered, our quarters were tight. He looked in both ways, then up and down, before stepping in.

"Close the door," I told him and he did so before turning to face me, hands behind his back and at attention like a wayward soldier.

"Do you know who I am?" I asked him, crossing my arms at my chest. He eyed my upper body, my face, my chest again, and then answered.

"Mr. Pebb," he said in a shaky voice, not matching his thick stature. "You're the boss."

"Right. I met Sheamus and I like him," I said wondering what the guy's reaction might be. I'd learn a lot from his next few words.

"Oh, yeah, Sheamus, he's great," he said in a rush.

"Who's he to you?" I asked, holding the guy's eye.

"Sheamus? Just a guy," Harry said with a nervous shrug. "He's a twink. He'd go out with you—he's easy."

The man's voice still quavered and I wondered why. I hadn't projected a threat in my posture. Why... Unless he felt guilty. I was done with him, ready to rejoin Sheamus.

"I'm moving him to another position and you won't see him again," I said and this time, allowed a narrowing of the eyes and a tiny step forward as an overt threat. "I'm

164

moving him under me, so I'll be near all the time. If you ever contact him again, I will know, and I will be angry." I lowered my voice at the last sentence and his mouth made a grimace trying to be a smile.

"Oh, sure, of course," he stammered. "He and I are nothing. Yeah, you'll like working with him. He's easy."

I narrowed my eyes further, in my imagination, the old Darcy surged into the guy, stabbed his throat and took his blood until that cocky asshole expression faded and died. But he saw enough disgust in my eye because he paled.

"Anything else, sir?" he whispered.

"You are a predator. I'll be watching you. If you prey on my employees again, I will know and I will prey on you."

Oh, that scared him. He blathered a few stupid phrases and I let him go. He wouldn't contact the kid again which was best for his health as well as employment. In another five minutes, I found the boy in the main lobby, his shift had ended but I had asked him to wait for me.

"Sheamus, you work under me, now, okay?" I told him and I put a hand to his shoulder. "Harry is not calling you back. Let me tell you about our holiday party…"

I indeed invited him to Cancun. Let's see what happened there.

12

My Straight CEO:

Round Two / Three's a Party

HEH-HEH, SHIT, WE DID NOT HAVE A THREE-WAY. I might have wanted to, but as a mortal, I don't always get what I want. I did think you'd enjoy hearing how it went with Chief and Sheamus during the Cancun week.

I took a separate jet to enable the grand entrances I'm so fond of. I had arranged a single scheduled meal with the boss and requested everyone attend with their plus-one. I remained out of sight as my employees settled into their villas, relaxed a bit, and then dressed for dinner.

At nine on the dot, I strode to the dining hall to find everyone seated at the long tables, chatting and nibbling appetizers. Each wore his or her finest clothes and I enjoyed the sparkle of the sequined gowns and the dramatic flair of the tailored tuxedos.

I entered as always, exuding confidence and sex—I am what I am. My guests stood and I motioned for them to sit, loving the way some of them petted me with their eyes as I reached my seat. I gave Chief a nod. I'd asked Kiki to sit him at least seven people down. This way, we could play the gaze game all night, which would be fun.

The man beside him turned then and I met eyes with my elevator friend. Sheamus beamed me a child-like grin and I gave him a wink. Had he chosen to bunk with Chief? I had instructed Kiki to find him someone compatible. This was good. Chief would help the kid discover his inner confidence. Good. Add to that, Sheamus already looked like a different man, his expression happy and not the least bit pensive. I began to think Chief's pep-talks may have already begun.

The first course was served, and I made small talk with my nearby guests. Periodically, I shot a look to Chief, who worked hard to not blush. As the CEO, he wasn't ready to sit quiet, either. Now and then, he'd insinuate himself into my conversations. One of these instances, I responded with a sultry look reminiscent of the way I must have looked at him while in bed together, for he cleared his throat and got to his feet. He excused himself and returned a few minutes later. I listened to my employees' banter politely, but inside, I started reliving that night, the evening I showed my CEO how a man can pleasure another man.

The final course was served around ten and no one had spoken of business within my hearing. I took in some of their glassy, sated expressions and got to my feet. In varying degrees of energy, everyone else stood as well, looking my way to ask the next imperative. I gave them a grin.

"You are on vacation, and this was the only scheduled event. Your boss is stepping next door where I will show any of you how to slow dance to 80's pop music." My board all chuckled and I read in a few eyes that they would take me up on it. This was fine. There's one thing I truly enjoy now that I'm mortal and that's the feel of a stranger under my palm. Dancing, shaking hands, hugging, anything where my hand conforms to a person's flesh gives me a thrill. I've thought of the reasons why and have landed on this—you guys are soft. Even when you buff out, there are parts of you so pleasant to touch and stroke. I spent so little time with mortals as Rakum, that I did not appreciate this before. Believe me when I tell you, I do now.

In the dance hall the music pounded high energy, so I headed to the bar. I would wait for a slow dance and I ordered a whiskey. Once the barkeep handed it over, I nodded to the man two stools down. He was one of the hired actors I'd contracted for the evening. This idea came from Kiki who worried that she wouldn't find anyone to play with since the resort was rented out exclusively to my company for the week. Now she had twenty strangers to choose from, and any leftovers might find a single among my available employees. It was about fun, and I paid these men and women to be nice. Anything else, I didn't need to know about.

"Are you Mr. Pebb?" the man asked, moving to one stool away and putting out his hand. I shook and said that I was. "Great party, man. Thank you for the invite."

"You're very welcome," I assured him. My mind went to the resumés the casting agent sent. Each performer created a role for him or herself and would play it for the gig. This one's name was Galahad and he'd devised a backstory of being a former child actor who now directs documentaries for the various history channels. I called him by his chosen moniker, revealing I'd read his dossier.

"Hah! That's right, yessir. Nice to meet you. Do you like history? I'm doing a Civil War project right now."

I gave him a dismissive nod, bored by the topic. The band started a slow ballad and he interested me with his next question.

"Want to dance?"

I wonder what my face revealed because he began backtracking, as if he misjudged something between us. I admit, I'm reworking my sexuality, considering heterosexual marriage. But I hadn't proceeded with it. I *did* want to dance with him, and I grinned and stepped off the stool for the dance floor.

"Great," he said stumbling over nothing. "Shit, thought I offended you..."

I chuckled and when we reached the other dancers, being taller, I put my hands to his shoulders and he put his to my waist. Looking into my face, he blushed after a minute and shook his head with chagrin.

"Why did you say yes? I know what I look like," he said in a laugh, speaking low.

I grinned again, both of us swaying in time with the music. The hall used a disco ball to throw sparkling light willy-nilly about the space and its people, and periodically, his green eyes flashed blue as I watched him. He wasn't unappealing. He was six feet with sandy blond hair, friendly eyes in a doughy physique. His humility and kindness bubbled from within and this is probably why I accepted the dance, but did I really need to explain myself?

When I hadn't verbally replied, he added, "Seriously. Your friends look pretty shocked." He made a show of glancing to the other people around on all sides.

"What are you asking me?" I had spoken softly, aware that the deep growl in my voice tickled his libido. I was not in seduction mode, but it comes out anyway.

He tried to guess something from my question, but I wasn't playing mind games. This is something mortals do, but I have no interest in mastering. The neutralized ish-mikhan ghost inside of me whispered he needed compliments. What the hell. I enjoyed his smile more than this worried expression he'd adopted once we started moving together. I leaned closer to speak in his ear and decided to let my tongue say whatever it pleased.

"Sometimes when a man accepts an invitation to dance, he simply enjoys your presence. Maybe he likes the way you look or speak or the polite way you asked..." I paused with drama, allowing my breath to fall on his ear. "Maybe he imagines what you might be like in bed, that maybe you're kind and gentle and the sort that makes sure your partner gets off first no matter what..."

His breath hitched and his chin jerked right as if to catch my eye. I leaned out enough to see and finished my thought just as quietly, but he read my lips well enough in the romantic music booming throughout the room.

"Don't question the boss." I gave him a new smile that melted his features. He leaned in to resume the dance, but the slow music had ended, the DJ starting up a pulsing new rhythm. I moved away to arm's length and invited him to join me at the bar. With round eyes, probably wondering where all that was going, he followed.

When we both had fresh whiskeys, we sat facing each other for conversation. This guy was safe. He wasn't yet thirty, seemed to have an interesting career and fun personality. Maybe he and Sheamus would hit it off. I had a protective feeling about that young man, maybe because of my past or maybe because of the disgusting pig that had been abusing him, but I wanted to see the kid happy. "Galahad" might be a fun one to know.

I touched his sleeve. "I want to introduce you to a friend of mine. A kid who works in my office."

He nodded and I looked at the crowd. Sheamus stood out because of his coloring and he grinned when I caught his eye. When he came close, I introduced him. The actor shook the boy's hand and asked if he liked history. I had to chuckle when Sheamus announced he was studying for a History major online. In another few moments, the two launched a new conversation about World War II and I eased away. What a funny guy. I'd ask the kid about it later, but I was hoping he had found a friend. Not for sex—honest—but for companionship. Someone he could share himself with that wouldn't take advantage of his gentle nature.

I was still pondering all this when I felt a tap on my shoulder. It was Chief and I knew it before I turned. He shook my hand, his left palm clapping my bicep.

"Boss-man, so good to see you. You look well," he said raising his voice on the last word. I reciprocated the same compliment, although the formal conversation was for everyone else's ears. He wanted to be alone with the boss. Whether that was my wishful thinking or true empathy, I asked him if he'd like to go for a walk.

"Sure," he said, and we headed out the exit with our hands in our pants pockets, just two businessmen on a moonlit stroll. A dozen strides into the warm ocean air and we shed our suit coats, draping them over our arms. We walked in silence for another minute until I removed my cufflinks and rolled my sleeves to my elbows. Chief's eyes cut my way, and with a tiny smirk, he mimicked my movements, pocketing his cufflinks and rolling up his own sleeves.

His forearms were decidedly more sculpted than nine months ago, and I said, "You've been working out."

He gave me a knowing grin. "Since I returned home from our drinking game. I guess you inspired me," he finished, a knuckle to my chest.

Without a care, I slowed to a halt and reached out to wrap my palm around his forearm. He'd been regular Army and a snake tattoo with military insignia decorated the area.

"Very nice," I said and raised my eye to his. I grinned at what I was about to say, I didn't (or couldn't) help myself. "I'd like to see more."

There it was, he blushed again. But something I hadn't expected—Chief didn't immediately jump on board. I realized my error, hell, I titled this chapter after the theme—Chief wasn't gay. Then or now.

Since seeing me in New York last year, he hadn't kissed a man. He had returned to his straight life. His straight friends. His straight future. I read this in his eyes. He was over the confusion and angst he experienced in my hotel room the night of the drinking game.

I sighed inside. If we were going to fuck, I was going to have to seduce him all over again. My mind turned to the forty-odd other people in residence I could approach, none of them requiring such effort. I wondered if chief saw some of this in my face, because he chuckled and resumed walking.

"I've been looking forward to this night," he admitted in a wistful tone, facing the breezy night ahead. Our pace had picked up and we were headed for his assigned villa. My hopes remained minuscule but alive.

"Did you want a new drinking game?" I asked, trying hard to be human.

He nodded once in an embarrassed huff. "When I got home, our game night seemed like a dream. The more time passed, the more I pretended it never happened." He shot me a kind glance and resumed looking forward. "I went back to work, you know, just good ol' Chief. Doing my thing. Over the summer, I started going back to church…"

"Ah," I said without planning to. We had reached his assigned rooms and he opened the door and asked me in, without a pause. I followed him in and we moved to the main room. He pointed a knuckle to the couch and turned for the mini-bar. I watched in silence as he gathered all of the tiny bottles and brought them in his untucked shirt, just as he had in New York. He settled beside me, half-a-cushion apart and dumped his bounty between us.

"You started going back to church and what?" I asked, allowing my voice to lower and slow down. I was beginning to think we'd do it. Maybe he would remove his shirt and show me how he developed his pecs.

He chuckled and handed me a Svedka. "I just started taking God seriously again. My daughter wants to be a preacher so…" he shrugged.

"What are you saying?" I asked in the same voice. "You're sending your pal some mixed signals and my machine is very difficult to wind down once it gets going."

Chief shot me a glance and looked back to the bottle in his hand. "I've given this a lot of thought; I want to play the game." He looked up and locked my gaze. "The same game. Same topic. Same rules."

Fuck. My CEO was back on the Rakum kick. But what could I do? If this is what it took to get him to lower his guard, bottoms up! I unscrewed my bottle and told him to go first.

"Is Corey Huffman one of your brothers?" he asked and guzzled down his mini without a problem. Huffman was head of security at Pebb headquarters. He's as tall as me, but that's as far as it goes. I guess Chief found him attractive. Heh.

"No," I said and realized I'd answered as if I was a Rakum. I followed up with, "if I was part of that dead race." He chuckled. "Okay, my turn," I said with humor and gurgled mine down. I'd had three glasses of wine with dinner and two whiskeys at the bar, so yours truly was feeling a bit giddy. "Do you want to fuck the boss again?"

Chief's eyes widened and he offered a nervous titter. "The rules say I can lie, remember?"

"Is that your next question?" I asked, entering full seduction mode, studying now his shape through that crisp white tuxedo shirt. Too fucking late, I had started the countdown with or without permission.

"No," he replied in a rush.

"No, what? No, it's not your next question, or no, you don't want to fuck the boss?" I asked, holding his eye with a sideways grin.

"Undecided," he said in a whisper and shook his head with a *shew*. "Come on, Boss," he said with muted humor. "You did this last time. Let me ask some questions before you turn on that voice." He did not look up for a long minute, but he was smiling. Then he said, "My turn," and knocked back another one. "How difficult has it been going from Rakum to mortal?"

Now I huffed. He'd done it again, like last time, asking something I couldn't answer with a single word. Instead of replying, I unscrewed another vodka and drank it down in three gulps. I licked my lips and trained my gaze to his top button.

"Open your shirt and I'll answer you truthfully," I said staring at the soft chest hair peeking out the collar. Then Chief's fingers were unbuttoning the shiny pearl-topped nubs, one after the other, until they were all undone. He flapped it open with drama. He was looking at my face, but I did not remove my eyes from his chest.

He was wearing a fucking undershirt, of course, and I wasn't getting the show I wanted. Still, his musculature had rounded with his resistance training, pecs pressing against the fabric, tight abs that did not protrude as they had our last rendezvous. In a languid manner, I raised my eye to his. At the same time, he held my gaze, unscrewed a new mini and drank it down.

"It's getting easier," I said in a whisper. "You're helping quite a bit." I gave him a new grin and he did nothing, just holding my eye, breathing a bit heavier, leaning back since removing his shirt. "New rule," I said even lower and as I had been sitting catty-corner to him on the couch, I rolled to a standing position looking down on him. "I'm too drunk to continue this way."

Chief licked his lips looking up at me, his eyes at half-mast. "I'm not drunk enough," he said matching my tone.

"F-u-u-u-c-k," I said dragging out the word.

I maneuvered to straddle his lap and dropped my weight atop his thighs. I uncapped a bottle from his stash and held it to his lips. My new game? Give him little truths until he was drunk enough to take me in.

"I came into the world in 1710, Moldavia…" I said in a gentle slur, my tongue reminding me to drink no more. Chief caught my drift and drank it down, a little more carefully than before. I grinned thinking how hard he was working to figure me out. I'd tell it all and deny it later; why not?

"Again," he said mostly mouthing the word.

With a grin and moving in slow motion, I handed him a new drink. What would he like to know now? My mind crawled along my memory of the Rabbit book that had alerted him to his boss's possible *supernaturalness.*

"I didn't know the Rabbit's husband," I began, and he nodded, showing me he followed. "But that Elder that marked her? I know him. Knew him. Whatever." I chuckled. "Fuck, Chief. Drink that shit down." I laughed softly and he drank it, also with a chortle.

Leaning into the cushion and looking up at my face, he shook his head in slow motion. "No mas. No mas." He giggled once and shook his head again, his palms coming up to drop to my thighs. He squeezed his fingers. "What now, Boss-man?" he whispered, finally allowing his eyes to fall to my shirtfront, then my middle, then my belt. "You're wearing a ton of layers."

I was, too. Remaining on his legs, I worked off my shirt and undershirt as he pulled his over his head to toss aside. I blinked trying to clear my vision, I was fucking close to passing out. I rubbed my eyes with one hand and across his strong chest with the other.

"The Puppeteer just wants us to be holy," he said in a soft whisper, slurring the last word.

"Holy moly," I said, but I heard him.

I had spent the past nine months also becoming

178

more familiar with the God who made me. I understood He had parameters regarding our behavior and how we treat one another.

Chief laughed at my re-use of his word and his fingers tucked into my waistband at the belt. Not going any further, just hooked there. He raised his gaze to mine. Once I knew he'd seen me checking him out, I met his eye.

"He wants us to listen to Him. To love one another…" he said in the same voice, again a bit slurred. I thought about the messenger at Last Assembly. The same tune, same song, now in my CEO's mouth. "Fuck, Darcy," he breathed, "you gotta stop doing that…"

I grinned. This was the first time he'd called me by my name. I didn't stop. I had scooched up and started a grind against his tented slacks that he couldn't ignore. "Or what?" I said low.

Chief's right hand shot to my neck and he tugged. Of course, I did not resist and our mouths touched. Oh, it was just like before, tentative, but sexy and masculine. Our kiss deepened and my brain was swimming by now. I had drank too much and I didn't stand up when Chief ended the kiss. He looked into my face, made a little "let's go" movement with his hips, but if I stood, I'd pass out. I shook my head and Chief gave me a kind grin.

"Do this," he said and after grabbing my shoulders, he pulled, aiming my upper body for the remainder of the extra-long couch. When I'd dropped into position, he got out from under my weight and fixed my legs out long. I watched all of this with my face to the cushion, your pal Darcy was almost out. My CEO pulled a soft blanket from the nearby recliner and draped it over me.

I'd screwed up. My wait was over, my sexy CEO was primed and half-naked, but the lights had dimmed. The last thing I heard before I was down for the count was Chief saying, "This trip is six nights long, Boss. Sleep tight."

Fuck.

I love that man.

I let the Sandman take me away. Chief was right. Damn, he was a great guy. Now you see why he's one of my favorite mortals, even today. Damn.

13

So, There You Have it

SO, THERE YOU HAVE IT – DARCY VANDIVER, the highlights of a very long and delightful life. If you only had the time to read more, I would have included various tales I cut for time and space. *It is my hope that you enjoyed the book.* I also hope you check out Jersey's other works. He puts me in as many as he can, but why not? I was there for much of his life. I was not in the first four books of The Rabbit Saga, but Jersey was mentioned often. The Elders that worked closely with that debacle (Roman and Kilmeade) had both favored Jersey in the past.

WHERE IS DARCY NOW? I'll save that for an upcoming novel, *The Vestige,* which will be the final installment of the Rabbit Saga story. I play a huge role in the plot of that book, so I better remain mum. Just trust me when I say, I am happy. I fathered children. And I fucked Elder Canaan … okay. Maybe I didn't, but I came so close. That's in *The Vestige*, so I'm going to hush.

Read on. I put a couple of delicious addendums up next. Hester tells us how he DIDN'T kill those breeders (sure) and then a little bit more of me.

Thank you for reading and if you enjoyed it, consider leaving a positive review on Amazon. They use those reviews to promote the book to other readers.

Kazak!

~ Darcy

14

Accidental Firebug

I had sent my pages to the editor when Jersey added this chapter of when Hester burned down the Breeder's Den. I alluded to it in my chapter, Hester, the Boil on My Ass, but Jersey thought it was too great to leave it for another book down the road. So here you go. Dive into the life of Hester. Roll up your sleeves; that one is sexy, alluring, really good at his job, but for day-to-day interaction? He's irritating as fuck. The end.

~ Darcy Vandiver

It was 1834 and I was only twenty when the fire killed those breeders. I didn't cause it. This is what happened.

~ Hester

"THERE HE IS!" Maven barked when I rounded the corner.

I'd been in the cellar checking the breeders. All four were in fine shape, none of them pregnant, but soon a Father would be by to do the deed. My job was to keep them healthy and mentally stable, which isn't a foregone conclusion once they enter the breeding program. A woman accustomed to sun and fresh air has to remain below ground, eat what I serve them, and then wait. Oh, and consent their blood. Until I hear down the line that a Father is *en route*, these bitches must pony their blood on demand. This makes me very lucky; not only do I have consenting females any time I wish, but it calls brethren to my door and *Judas Priest!* This is a lonely assignment for a fix-it man.

So back to Maven. This soldier is my main companion, the only captain assigned to the breeder's den, and he's constantly horny. This works for me since I am, too. And I like his look – imagine a solid marble statue of a Roman Gladiator.

Now imagine him nude.

He-he. Sadly, Maven's rarely nude. He likes to make parts of him available and leave me gasping for more. What an asshole. Now that I write it down, he's a total shit to keep me in such a state of want. But, what can I say? He's my master – they all are. Keep in mind, at this time, I was only twenty years old and had not yet met a younger Rakum. That put me at the bottom of the totem pole. The end.

If Darcy didn't already tell you, Rakum don't mature sexually until around a century old. Their body works—they are able to come erect—but true desire won't arise until almost a hundred. For ish-mikhan, our sex drive comes around *very young*—sometimes as soon as we can wrap our tiny hands around our dick. Just trying to help. You're welcome. Goo.

I was born here, proselytized here by Elder Blu, and I've never left, even for an overnight trip. This is not unusual; I'd live a thousand years, suck my brothers off a million times, and travel every continent before I turn to dust, so big fucking deal. Darcy wanted me to give my side of the firebug story, so I'll focus down on that. If he would allow me to pontificate on my love life, I'm sure I could entertain you more than he can. Think about it—he's enormous. He can't possibly fix Elders better than I can. Everything about me is proportional and perfect—no one would consider me a freak, which I'm sure our brothers feel about Darcy.

Hey, giraffe-boy, just because you haven't heard any complaints, doesn't mean they don't subconsciously prefer Hester over your towering ass.

I apologize for the rant. I read some of this book when they asked me to contribute a chapter. Darcy's in love with Darcy—that's all you need to know.

So, Maven.

My brother called me close and I hopped to attention. My station allows me to dictate sexual matters no matter what Rakum is involved and I exploit that power to the limit, which makes up for being the youngest turd in the bowl.

Maven whistled, requesting I move faster. "Sit on my lap, Ishy. I gotta show my boys what a fantastic little fucker you are."

Expressionless but flattered, I got close enough for Maven to scoop me into his lap. I'm no shrimp—5'10" and growing (I'd top out at 6'), but he's 6'4" and lords it over anyone shorter. He tucked me onto his thighs facing the two brothers, my knees apart and hanging in midair. He wrapped me up around the middle and rested his chin on my shoulder, his eyes to his inferiors.

"Echo, Stark, meet Hester, my special friend," he said, his deep voice tickling my ear. His closeness revved my engine and for the time being, I resisted. He wanted something novel; I listened to my muse and waited to see what it was. Something would please him and I'd weed it out soon enough.

"He's pretty as a woman," the one called Stark said. I met his eye with a smirk. I'm prettier than any mortal, male or female, and he knew it. I think they like to toy with my pride, and I work to avoid taking the bait.

"But is he as soft as a woman?" Echo asked and rose from his seat to walk close.

As his hand stroked my cheek, I garnered Maven's need; he wanted these two men to marvel at his good fortune, to thank him for sharing his ish-mikhan. Here it was—my duty and I would not fail.

One down, two to go.

A fix-it man serves by knowing what the Rakum wants before he does. I had figured out Maven, so I turned my full diagnosis to Echo. All I needed to do was move and allow my muse to do the rest, so I did.

"Do you fuck a lot of women?" I asked Echo.

186

The question garnered a laugh from Stark and Maven, but my attention was on Echo. He didn't laugh—this was the start of his *fixing* and part of him knew it. With a smooth movement, I slipped off my master's lap and stepped into Echo's space, looking up at him, my eyes drinking in his wide shoulders and bushy bearded cheeks.

"Catch me." I said in his mind and darted away.

I had a destination in mind—my quarters—which were clear across the underground compound. Echo would catch me; I couldn't outrun him. But my muse demanded this course, so I pumped my legs as hard as I could and Echo accepted the challenge. I heard his footfalls milliseconds behind me. Our brethren remained in the kitchen and I was three-quarters to my bedroom when I was violently shoved to the ground from a flat-out sprint.

"You're it," Echo said standing over me, his hands to his hips and seeking my eye. "What are you thinking? How could you outrun me? You've barely been alive five minutes and I'm three hundred years old."

I pretended to be winded, lying on my back looking up at him, forcing labored breathing like a mortal. I still didn't look into his eyes. Instead I made sure he saw me checking out his shape from his thick neck and wide shoulders, a thick muscled middle, and my gaze stopped at his crotch. Hidden behind that layer of cotton was his pride and joy.

Echo looked down to his own lap. He arranged himself left, right, up and down. He looked back at me. "What are you up to?"

The puzzlement in his face spoke to my muse: *he has never slept with the ish-mikhan.* Ah, this was precious to me and I gave him a small grin and met his eye.

"Hester, what's this? I thought we would fuck or something. Why am I chasing you?"

I put out my hand and he pulled me to my feet. I stumbled into him, a fake loss of balance, and he caught my upper arms, stabilizing me and setting me on my feet. My muse is a genius because the man's eyes grew soft—I was fixing him already and we hadn't even undressed.

I lifted my foot a few inches and looked down. When he also looked down, I rotated my ankle and faked a wince. Before I faced front again, Echo's strong hands to my arms, he bent low and picked me up, holding me before him.

"Which door, this one?" he asked walking briskly down the way we had been moving. I held my "injury" out and nodded. The brother made entry, kicked the door closed behind him, and walked to my mattress. With more care than I expected, he set me down, arranged my head on the pillow and stood erect. He unbuttoned his shirt, looking upon me, and watching to see if I'd speak or do something else silly, like pretending to sprain my ankle.

…How ludicrous…

That word came from his mind, but as I watched him undress, his boots and socks, and then his slacks, his mind also pondered my beauty, my symmetry, the utter perfection in every line. I batted my eyelashes and he grinned.

"Do I fuck a lot of women," he mumbled low, repeating

what he'd heard me say. I put out both hands and he took them, collapsing atop me a moment, long enough to kiss my mouth, and then he slid to one side. "Yes, as a matter of fact, I do."

Echo used the fingers of one hand to unbutton my shirt and I helped him wiggle it free. He started at my pants and I helped him slide those off, too.

"You're being one of those women, aren't you? That's what ishys do, right? This is what I need. Is that right?"

I only grinned, the face of a man who needed more kisses, and Echo obliged. As my muse directed, I allowed Echo to lead the dance, following and filling in anywhere he fell off. But he was having a blast—loving me like he loved those women.

Why the hell would I do that?

Because our brethren don't tolerate that shit. We'll fuck each other for our personal reasons, but none of us will fake weakness, pretend to be mortal to help our partner be fulfilled.

But an ish-mikhan will.

Echo will never in his life sleep with another Rakum that gives him the pleasure I did that night. He was allowed to be himself, brutish, rough, a full Rakum captain, and he couldn't hurt me. I'm a brother and I can take it, all of it, and I wanted it. I let that fucker use my body for nearly an hour. Much longer than Stark would need, and never did Maven go more than ten minutes. Maybe he would after tonight—he's going to want to hear from this brother what a great time he had, and my roommate is going to be jealous.

When I saw fit to let him release, he did with more gratitude than I'd seen in a brother in my short lifetime. If I had been older and in charge of my life, I'd have kept him in my bed another night, gone another round. But none of this was possible, so when he'd come and held me close another five minutes, he dressed and left. He was amazed at me and he went to send Stark in my direction.

I was happy. I didn't wash up; my genius muse informed me the man would prefer the comfort of sweat and sex and blood—oh. Stark wanted violence. I saw it all clearly as he approached my door. I hopped up and by the time he pushed into the room, I brandished my dagger. Stark grinned to one side and jerked a larger knife from the small of his back.

It's okay. I like this, too.

Game on.

Maven tiptoed into our room and I watched with sleepy eyes as he came to my side. He leaned low and grabbed my chin with two fingers. I was half-asleep, but since he pressed his mouth to mine and forced his tongue to my palate, I rolled over and reached for his shoulders.

"Nuh-huh," he mumbled and pushed us apart. He stood back up and I dropped onto the bed. "You make me proud— these brothers will be talking about this night for decades."

I grinned with a single nod.

"You have the duty," he said and backed away. I watched him leave and put my feet to the floor. My internal clock told me the sun was down and if Maven turned the watch to me, he would be gone all night, maybe longer. I always took care of the breeders, but the duty included guarding the place from mortals and wild beasts.

I sponged off; the delightful aromas of my brothers needed to be erased no matter how much I enjoyed them. By the time I assumed Maven's post—the windows of the exterior doors—it was full dark and the entire facility was still as the dead.

Wait. It was too still.

I didn't hear the breeders. They are usually speaking to one another through the thin room walls, or calling to me for something or other.

Wait. I didn't hear their *hearts.*

I looked backward down the dark hallway. If I leave to check them, I'd be leaving the doors unguarded. How many intruders do we have any given evening? None. I could risk a peek at the females. I wondered what to do and had to laugh when I realized my muse sucked at guard duty.

Then I smelled smoke.

I abandoned the doors and headed below, deep underground, three more levels where we kept the Fathers' females. They all had candles and lanterns, fireplaces and whatever a woman might need to see in the dark. What had they done? What carelessness could have caused the growing acrid aroma in the air?

When I reached the breeders' level door, I opened it and a wall of smoke rolled over me. Rakum can hold their breath for ages, so I did and surged into the hazy spaces. I saw no flame, but the closer I got to female #2's door, the hotter the air grew.

I smelled cooked flesh just before I swung open her room access.

She was dead. Burned to death by a fire it looked like she started. The rooms have no windows to the outside, but they had glass openings to see their fellow breeders. This glass was broken to #1's room and through the film of gray, I saw that room was also free of flame.

I pulled a torch from the wall, lit it, and searched for clues. There were four women in residence, and I sensed all four had died. My search turned up no flame and I moved back to the stairwell and propped open the door. On each level, I propped open doors and at the top, I forced the trap door to stay open as well.

I called to Maven in his mind, *"The breeders are dead. There's been a fire."* My master sent back a slew of expletives and a threat to turn me over to the Fathers for reeducation.

Hey, it wasn't my fault. I'm writing this chapter centuries later so I can tell you what I later determined.

Breeder #2 was an accidental firebug. (Hey, Darcy, it wasn't me, asshole. I did my duty…) The evidence revealed that she'd been adjusting the kindling and set the bedlinens on fire. She was unable to get the flame out before she succumbed to suffocation, and then her body burned along with the cloth in the room. The structure is stone and dirt, so once the fire consumed the cloth, it petered out. Because #2 had broken the windows to #3, the smoke suffocated them too. And #4 broke through to #3 probably to help her and she also died of asphyxiation.

192

None of this was my fault.

Had I not been guarding the front, I still would have been on a different level entertaining my master. No matter how anyone looks at it, I didn't cause this.

So, Darcy, *suck-it.*

Now, let's discuss my memoir. Jersey said he'd turn my writings into a memoir like he did for you. Come on. I want to tell my story. Put in a good word for me with Jersey. I'll make it worth your while, you delicious oaf.

~ Hester

Malcontent

A SNEAK PEEK into Emil's newest novel…

*"You'd enjoy learning that **Malcontent** contains a few sex scenes between me and Pitch. Oh, I miss him…*

"AFTER WE WENT MORTAL, a psychotherapist named Ruth Angleton (who lives with her Rakum lover, K'fir) is treating anger issues in my old friend Pitch (remember him / Tole chapter?) when someone begins killing transgendered women. It's a vampire / serial killer / thriller, and **yours truly** *shows up in Chapter Eight.*

"You must realize by now that if I share a chapter, it'll be the one that introduces me. Enjoy it as if flipping television channels and stopping on a compelling movie scene.

"I can't help it; Jersey wrote me in SO FINE." ~ Darcy

[Set-up: NOVEL IS FROM RUTH'S PERSPECTIVE. Ruth hates Christians, her Rakum lover might be converting; her anger-management former-vampire patient (Pitch) takes her to the special Rakum church to spy on her lover and see what they're up to in there...]

Chapter 8 Church with Pitch

Not too surprisingly, the guards at the church gate let us through. Pitch didn't recognize the Rakum, but he said the right words in their language. In as much as I could see in the darkened landscape, I marveled at the meticulous care given to every shrub, tree, and curb. White criss-cross horse fencing lined both sides of the drive causing me to want to see it in the day—maybe they had horses. I'm not a rider, but what little girl doesn't dream of a black stallion to solve all her woes?

The church cube sat illuminated by LED lamps directed to its four corners and front door. The parking slots lined both sides and our driver let us out, intending I guess to pull around and wait for us to be finished. Pitch and I both made meaningless remarks before we stood at the entrance prepared to enter. With a tiny glance at my face, he pushed inside, walking without checking the occupants ahead of him. I paused maybe three seconds, holding the door open and peering into

the gigantic room. Kiefer was nowhere in sight.

"Ah! It's Pitch!" a man's voice barked and approached without meeting my eye. He got right into Pitch's face and swung a left hook. Maybe for a millisecond I thought a negative event had occurred, but I recovered having learned this was a proper greeting among many of them. If they didn't screw, they greeted each other with violence. If they spent their together time in the sack, they used a gentler greeting.

"You look well, muthfukka," Pitch said, pronouncing the curse with humor as he dodged the offender's blow and delivered a vicious upper cut to his chin. The strike made contact and his brother spiraled backward, laughing and bringing one hand to his face even as he tumbled ass-down to the tiled floor. The man on the floor glanced at me and asked Pitch a question in their language. Thankfully, Pitch answered in English, translating, which was nice.

"This is Kfir's mate. Where's he hiding?" Pitch asked and didn't help the Rakum to his feet. I watched him scramble to standing position, massaging his jaw as he continued the conversation.

"Unloading some shit with Walker." The so-far-un-named Rakum hooked a thumb backward and looked to me. "Kfir's woman…" He turned to Pitch and finished in their language. I interpreted the tone—he didn't like me or humans or women.

As I had grown accustomed, they spoke several minutes in Rakum Hungarian as if I didn't exist. I let my mind wander. I didn't feel comfortable walking away, so from where I stood, I put my hands behind my back and simply drank it in. I studied the other men in the place, the bema at the front, and the floor

196

and the ceiling. I was about to start the circuit all over again when a mountain of something amazing walked in from a back hall.

It was a man—a Rakum—but there was something different about him. I'll break it down. He swaggered in, truly, as if in his mind, everyone was watching, adoring, and worshipping him. I think I was the only one looking, and wait… I guess I worshipped him a little, studying his walk, his build, the way his hair hung to his chin and swayed with each step. Holy shit, his profile and then ¾-face had my stomach doing flip-flops. He stopped at a collection of his brothers, stood three and four inches over all of them. He nodded and chuckled and although I couldn't hear his voice, his laugh was deep. One of his brothers lifted a hand to his neck and squeezed. The Adonis's reaction was to lean down to press his face in. From my angle, it could have been a whisper, a kiss, or a bite, but he held their faces like that a few seconds.

Oh, fuck.

He looked up and locked eyes with me.

This man had yellow eyes—no shit. Even from twenty yards, they shimmered as if they were supposed to be hazel but ended up without enough melatonin. Whatever the cause, they were bright. I nodded reflecting his movement and he started toward me. With my eyes wide, I glanced at Pitch. He was still engaged with the man he hadn't introduced. Sexy eyes had reached me and he put out a hand.

"My name is Darcy," he said and I loved his voice with my whole heart. "You're surely not with Pitch, so…" he said and when I gave him my hand, he lifted it and tenderly pecked the outside. "What's your story?"

I offered a polite smile and in my peripheral vision, Pitch noticed and closed his conversation. He turned to put his arm about my shoulders and face the taller man.

"Move along, Vandiver," Pitch said and rolled his hand. "She has enough _____" Pitch finished in their language. *Darcy Vandiver.* Now I had his entire name and it seemed to rhyme in my head.

"I'll take you to Kfir," he said with a bow, putting out one elbow in a gesture you might see in a black and white film. I didn't accept. He was accustomed to yes, so I tossed him a no. His brow lifted and he smiled. "You prefer I move along?" he asked, his voice indicating he'd do it. He didn't need me and was only being polite. I remembered he was a Rakum and answered forthrightly.

"I'll wait with Pitch. Thanks."

The man's smile remained, and he held my eye two more seconds. Then he nodded in a graceful and tiny bow before turning away. I watched him go, every cell in my body wanting to know him better. Kiefer entered and they met as he walked my way. I watched for their greeting—touch. Ah. And a kiss to the jaw. Shit. Another man I should wonder if my lover's sleeping with. Kiefer passed him and met my eye with a new grin.

"What is this?" he asked, his eyes jumping between mine and Pitch's. When he was close enough, he greeted me in the mortal fashion – pecked my mouth and slid his hand down my arm from bicep to wrist to hold my fingers as we spoke. This was progress.

"Pitch offered to bring me. This is very interesting," I said with a glance to each corner. "This is where a Rakum meets God."

Kiefer chuckled once and his eyes flashed with humor (or maybe it was affection. I am not as sure with this new thing he's doing). "Let me introduce you around," he said and turned away, holding my hand.

Then, for fifteen minutes, my boyfriend walked me through the groups, speaking English, and his brethren followed his lead. Pitch did not join us, but disappeared to do his own thing. When Keifer and I had made the circuit, he stopped at the front near a podium and the one called David Walker approached.

"And here's David," Kiefer said and I gave the man a nod. As I noted when I saw him in the photo; I'd never seen any Rakum like him before. I suppose the oddest thing, Rakum-wise, was his expression. He just looked *sweet*. If I'd seen him first out in the world, I never would have pegged him as a Rakum.

After he made a comment regarding the schedule, he grinned and caught my eye. "Say it," he said in a laugh. "Your face…"

Keifer turned to see my expression and his brow lifted. "Yes, what is it?"

Amazed that I was so easy to read I waved one hand. "I was thinking you look nothing like a Rakum. I don't mean it as an insult, but I've met probably a hundred, and you, well…" I shrugged one shoulder, but as I expected, the man was not offended.

"Ah," he said with a knowing grin to Keifer. "I never fit in with my brothers. Now that I follow the Maker, I realize He made me this way for a purpose."

Keifer nodded in agreement but I didn't want to remark. Nothing about church or God interested me in the least.

"We just finished the service," David said allowing the previous topic to drop. "Do you want to sit-in on some small groups? Kfir tells us you're a doctor of psychiatry and work to help my brothers assimilate. I would enjoy being part of that. Perhaps we can share contact information. If a brother comes to either of us for something we can help with, we'll refer them over."

"Like if he's sociopathic, you'll send him to me, and if he wants to know about God, send him to you?" I asked in what I thought sounded like a polite tone.

Walker nodded with a friendly smile. "Precisely." He tipped a chin to Pitch. "Be cautious spending your time with him. Kfir informed me of his promise regarding you, but he's not trustworthy." David turned his face to Keifer. "Does she know his specialty before?"

Keifer took my hand in his. "Pitch is a seduction and torture expert. Men and women the master wanted chastised or ended, Pitch would be sent to draw them close enough to grab without attracting authorities." With a gentle grin, Kiefer lifted his hand to move my hair behind my ear. "But he will not break his vow to me, meaning he won't touch you without consent."

"If you consent," David Walker added stepping in and lowering his voice, "he won't be gentle. If you were his mate instead of Kfir's, he'd prefer to rape you violently than make love. Do you understand what I am saying? For however long your association persists, he will seek to seduce and conquer you—his way."

I squirmed under their scrutiny, Keifer and David Walker both waiting for me to answer in the affirmative, that I wouldn't trust him, I promise, etc. And I believed them, *but they're working me so hard...* I nodded and a movement to the back door caught my attention. I looked over and Darcy Vandiver had reentered. In the three seconds in my gaze, his bright eyes flicked up and he sent me a nod. Shit, my blood rushed downward and I jerked my head to the side.

"I appreciate that, but I told Keifer, I don't want Pitch to touch me, *ever,*" I said and shook my head. "Anyway, I have a boyfriend." I looked up to Keifer who smiled and brought me into his chest.

"That's right." He leaned down to kiss my forehead.

"You left this in the shitter," a man's smooth voice sounded behind me and I turned my face. I thought it was Ivan, and I'd been right. He handed Keifer a Bible. But he'd come from outside, the front parking lot. Was it Ivan putting my love up all this time? Were they sleeping together?

Goddammit, Ruth!

I tightened my lips; he needed to come home.

"So, when will you be home?" I asked with the softest eyes I could muster.

"I don't know yet," he answered with a glance to Walker. "Not this week."

I huffed and did not hide it well. I would need to be straight; Rakum did not understand mind games. I ordered my thoughts. Think about it; females don't speak forthrightly. It doesn't come naturally or easily; everything we say and do has an ulterior motive. Not that its bad or good, its simply the way we're built. We must protect the treasure we keep between our legs, and protecting that treasure involves careful control of the dicks around us.

I took a deep breath and said in an even, non-emotional tone, "I want you to come home now. I want you to study this God thing a different way so we can be together every night like before. I don't like this separation."

Keifer gave me a thoughtful nod, his eyes dancing between Walker, Ivan, and me.

"Do the mortal thing and come home," I said as if the topic was closed.

"The mortal thing?" Keifer asked and his eyes narrowed.

"*F-u-u-u-c-c-k-k-k,*" Pitch said with mock exasperation walking into our circle. "Come on, doll-face. I'll run you back. Kfir will be home when he gets home. I think we've heard enough of this fairytale shit."

"David's right, baby," Keifer said to me and I met his eye. "I'll only take as long as necessary. I want to be with you, too. I miss you." He made a tiny grin and cupped my cheek. "That sounds like a great human sentiment and I really mean it."

"I know you do," I said, defeated. "Just hurry."

The four of us made a turn and started for the front doors of the large space while Ivan went the opposite direction. A few of the others called goodbyes to Pitch and in another minute we were in the lot watching the hired car drive into position to load up.

Keifer took me into his arms and hugged me, his chin resting atop my head. I held on, my arms around his ribcage, my fingers spread to take miniscule examinations of his muscular back. I hadn't had sex in four days, and that was a long time for us. Since I met Keifer, he was never short on libido.

But, his embrace turned platonic and when I turned up my face for a kiss, the peck he offered lasted less than a millisecond. When the driver opened the back door and I piled in with Pitch directly behind, I sat in the bench seat to watch Kiefer through the window. He had already turned, the goodbyes done, and was entering the building.

God, I hate that church, I said inside and maybe under my breath, because Pitch huffed what sounded like agreement.

(End Peek)

For a quick link to purchase MALCONTENT, visit www.emiljersey.com where he put it on the first page. ~ Darcy

You can read more about Darcy Vandiver in the following novels:

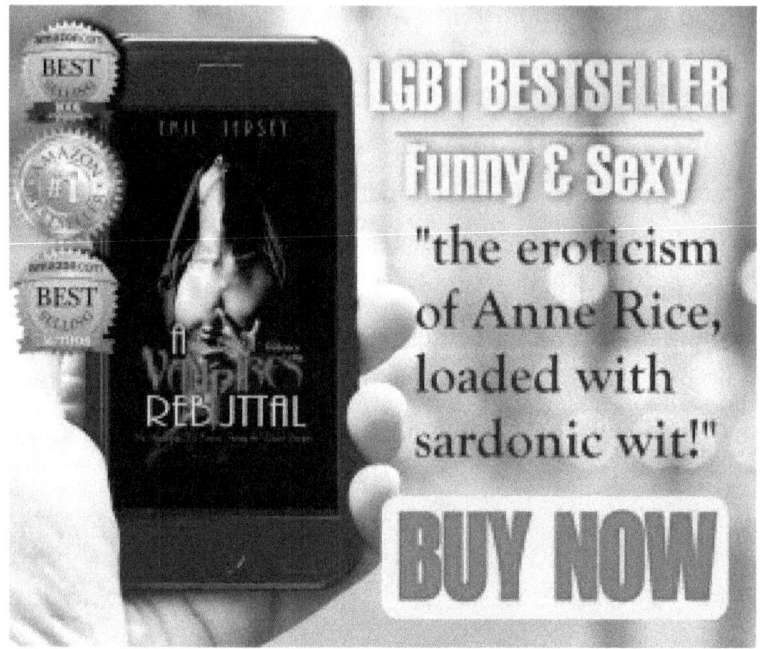

Blood Sex & Violence, a Vampire's Rebuttal by Emil Jersey (Run Rabbit Books 2019--MATURE)
www.emiljersey.com

Conundrum: The Lost Rabbit by Ellen C Maze (Little Roni Publishers 2019--MATURE) www.ellencmaze.com

Malcontent by Emil Jersey (Run Rabbit Books 2020--MATURE)

Where the Rabbit Characters were born...

140 5-star Reviews Across the Series
RABBIT EARNED FIVE READERS' FAVORITE SILVER SEALS!
Each book in the series also won a 5-star Silver Seal from ReadersFavorite.com!

(2020 Special Edition eBook Cover)
Rabbit: Chasing Beth Rider Book One of the Rabbit Saga

Ellen C Maze
13+, L S V
99 cents on Kindle
(Paperback price varies.)

JOIN THE CHASE
Rabbit: Chasing Beth Rider by Ellen C. Maze
#1 Top-Rated in Horror/Occult by Amazon Readers
Visit the author at www.ellencmaze.com, to sign up for her newsletter.
Twitter: @authorellenmaze
Visit the publisher at www.littleronipublishers.com/Run-Rabbit-Books.php

The Night Jersey Went Human from his novel/memoir, Blood, Sex & Violence, a Vampire's Rebuttal.

Jersey says:
"Here is where you will read about what happened the night I transformed into a mortal. This is from my memoir, but it's shortened for Darcy's book."

Going Human ~ Try Not to Kill Your Brother

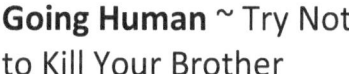

2017

Shirtless and relaxing alongside Avi on the couch, Jersey rubbed his belly in an absent manner, eyes on the television. Winston had pulled up a horror movie and for the moment, the nude teenagers on the cement floor hadn't noticed the monster bugs in the shadows. He and his brethren had fed well, locating a transient behind the burned-out paper mill, and now they sipped beers, full and comfortable, awaiting the sun. *Three hours until sunup,* Jersey counted inside, as every Rakum knew at a cellular level where the sun sat on its track.

Still rubbing his middle, enjoying the tickle of the hair to his palm, Jersey flicked his eye to Win. The brother sat in a recliner cattycorner to he and Avi on the sofa, his face to the TV. Onscreen, a mutant insect crawled into the breasty teen's hair as her boyfriend rammed into her with gusto. Jersey watched her nipples, his mind wandering to the last woman he fucked as his own hand fell still. The Cows were gone, but females still found him beautiful. If he fancied a pussycat, he knew where to find one. Presently, Avi's left palm assumed the task of rubbing Jersey's stomach in similar circles and Jersey grinned without turning. Avi preferred men and Win would fuck a cantaloupe—anything moist and warm inside suited his tastes. Once on a bet, he'd seen Win screw a horse. Jersey pivoted his eyes to Winston's profile. When it came to sex the biggest difference between the three of them was only Jersey refused to force sex. He didn't mind if they raped the entire city, but why do something he didn't want to do? He had no master. Part of their shitty new existence meant each man was on his own.

"That's a good boy, goooooooood boy," Avi cooed, moving his gentle and rhythmic stroking toward Jersey's waistband. He allowed the fingers to intermittently break the barrier and come back out toward his sternum. Jersey gave him a wink and looked back to the screen.

Winston turned at their movement. "Watch the movie, shit!" he hissed and faced front again.

Avi instead rolled onto his left which made petting easier. He put more ardor into each pass and leaned close to bury his face in Jersey's neck. "Let's go to bed, baby doll," he whispered between soft kisses.

Jersey still faced the movie and a scream erupted as a horde of alien roaches covered the woman's tits and she disappeared. The young man with her was saved the embarrassment of showing his junk eaten up by bugs as the camera panned away, on to the next scene. Avi had worked his mass in front of Jersey's right shoulder so Jersey brought that arm to rest around his brother's upper back. Winston looked at them again and gained his feet. He stomped to the couch and looked upon Jersey, hands to his hips.

"You requested this idiotic movie," he drawled with a thumb to the television. "If you're gonna fuck anyone, it's gonna be me. It's my turn, Avi, and I will break you in two if you try to jump the line."

Avi did not lift his face from Jersey's jaw and said against his skin, "Chill out. I'm only getting him primed up for you."

Jersey grinned, it was a good game having his roommates focus their energy on him. He watched for Win's reaction. With a slow blink and a twitch in his cheek, Win turned away for the basement.

"I'm hitting the shower. And Jerz, you sure as fuck better be down there in seven minutes. Got it?" He left without a reply.

Jersey would go—it was their game. He loved being adored and even though they could all sleep together—and they had—sometimes it was nice to be singularly attended.

"I thought he'd never leave," Avi said in his throat, now slurping his tongue around Jersey's earlobe. They had lived together two years and his brethren had learned his buttons. Jersey's right palm sat quiet against Avi's shoulder blades and he rest his left flat to the cushion. Let Avi do all the work, it was his turn anyway.

The shower went on in the basement where they would sleep the day away from the sun. If he was headed down, he needed to go. Reading his surface thoughts, Avi rolled even more over his left and draped his right leg across Jersey's thighs.

"Let's piss him off," he said low in Jersey's ear. Without asking, his fingers unbuckled Jersey's belt and began with the button. "We can end this night in an all-out brawl."

"Sounds good," Jersey whispered, now closing his eyes and Avi went to work lower, perfection in his every suckle, squeeze, and lave. His brother made a sudden change in the play by hopping up to straddle Jersey and look him in the face.

"Let's make this work," he said in Jersey's eye, and with a mischievous grin he thrust his pelvis once. Jersey smiled too and his brother swooped in to lock their mouths.

Then the universe flipped upside down.

Jersey flushed from his forehead to his toes in a cascading wave of nausea, jerking backward into the sofa cushion, his actions unintentionally knocking Avi to the floor. The room grew darker and the television brighter as a heavy stone grew where Jersey normally felt his stomach. It was fifteen long seconds before he gathered his wits enough to look at his brother on the floor. Avi's eyes were enormous.

"What the shit?" Avi hissed. Shaking hands palpated his own chest, his face, and then he propped onto his knees to shove a hand down his pants and examine his genitals. "What's wrong with me? Say something. I think I'm going deaf!" Avi inhaled, his fear evident.

Fear? SHIT!

Jersey shook his head in a tiny movement and pressed his palms to his body in a similar manner. The answer to Avi's question whispered across his subconscious and he screamed inside, *No way. No way. No way. No...fucking...way...* When their third brother shouted, "WHAT THE FUCK!" in the basement, Jersey stood tucking his ruined erection into his jeans and re-securing his belt. When he turned for the hall, he halted after one step. His body felt heavy, as if he'd donned a suit of armor. He forced another step, and then another, and behind him Avi followed posing his questions to the air.

"Shut up, Avi! Just SHUT UP!" Jersey belted aware that he had not yelled at either brother in anger since they met.

Anger? SHIT!

Stark naked and dripping water, Winston approached as they reached the basement floor. He met Avi's and then Jersey's eye, shaking his head side to side.

"No way," their brother said and reached Jersey to put a hand to his chest. Win cupped, squeezed, and prodded the muscle of Jersey's upper body and then his own, still mouthing, "no way."

"What? What is it?" Avi said in a high-pitched voice. "What's happening?"

Jersey put his hands to Winston's body and in a similar manner, rotated around to examine the broad surfaces of his muscled back.

"What? Judas Priest!" Avi said, near panic.

Panic? SHIT!

Fear, anger, panic – his inner mind listed off emotions, emotions Rakum did not possess.

"We're mortal," Jersey said in a very small voice his eye coming to rest in Winston's. "Fucking mortal."

"Mortal," Winston said just as low, holding Jersey's gaze with ferocity. Avi began to screech, exclaiming there must be another explanation, but Jersey and Win had no doubt.

"What do we do? What do we do? Who did this? WHAT THE SHIT IS GOING ON?" Avi's queries crescendoed and Winston clocked his jaw with a vicious right hook.

"Shut your hole, Avi, or I'll smash your face in!" he barked standing over his brother.

Avi had landed on his back and he remained there, eyes trained to the dark ceiling where a single bulb threw 40 watts of light across the basement. Blood ran from the side of his mouth—it wasn't red, but it also wasn't Rakum-black.

Winston lifted his fist, rotated it to see his knuckles. The skin split over the first and second joint, seeping a similar half-n-half fluid from the wound. Jersey stepped into him and taking the hand in his fingers, lifted the blood to his lips. He tasted it and when it had rolled around his palate a few seconds, Win tasted it too.

"What?" Avi said in a whisper, his fingers smudging the trickle on his face and then bringing the sample to his tongue.

Jersey's bloodlust had disappeared; he knew it down to his deepest parts. The metallic flavor of his brother's blood should have at least tickled his hunger, but nothing happened. From his housemates' expressions, they sensed the same thing.

"Winston," Avi said then, using a voice they had only heard in mortals. A sound of terror and impending death.

Win looked to Jersey. "You're the master," he whispered, piling the responsibility upon the oldest among them. "Now what?"

Jersey held his eye three long seconds, his mind as clear as ever, his memory as sharp, his intellect intact. They all knew of brethren who had turned mortal on purpose, accepting the yoke the Rabbit Beth Rider offered them at Last Assembly, but it had been voluntary. Why had the three of them turned human at such a random moment?

Jersey blinked and put a comforting palm to Win's shoulder. The sun was upon them, the house upstairs locked down. For the next eight hours, he and his two brothers would hash it out, phone Rakum they knew, get to the bottom of the issue. Jersey put out a hand to Avi and jerked him to his feet. By sundown, they'd have an answer, and if Avi could keep his cool, they wouldn't have to kill him before then. First order of business? Jersey brought both men close with his arms across their shoulders. It was mortal. It was a hug. But somehow, it gave them courage to face what lay ahead.

Visit www.emiljersey.com to learn more to purchase this sexy and fun vampire memoir!

---

[1] The Rakum race and our adventures are chronicled in a series entitled, **The Rabbit Saga Books** 1-6 by Ellen C Maze, and various add-ons in **The Rabbit Saga Collection.** https://www.emiljersey.com/The-Rabbit-Saga-Collection.php

[2] Namely, *Rabbit: Chasing Beth Rider* by Ellen C Maze, Little Roni Publishers, 2020. Ellencmaze.com